The Farfalle Fatality

A ROMANO'S FAMILY RESTAURANT COZY MYSTERY
BOOK 4

ROSIE A. POINT

The Farfalle Fatality

A Romano's Family Restaurant Cozy Mystery Book 4

Cover by DLR Cover Designs
www.dlrcoverdesigns.com

 Created with Vellum

Or simply search for me on *www.bookbub.com* and follow me there.

I look forward to getting to know you better.

Let's get into the story!

Yours,
Rosie

One

"THE MORETTIS COULD *NEVER*..." THE WORDS traveled through the interior of Romano's Family Restaurant, and a few diners in the space paused, turned their heads or arched eyebrows.

The woman at table number seven was a family friend. Thea Wakefield wore her dark hair in a pixie cut and had grabbed the seat at the head of the table the minute my server, Violet, had brought her party to their table.

A party of ten was a regular occurrence in Romano's, especially now that the chill of fall had set in and people wanted to spend more time with loved ones and friends eating good food. But a party of ten led by Thea was the stuff of legends.

Thea Wakefield had become infamous in Lake Basil over the past year. She was a gossip, a friend, a confidante

—if you kept in mind that talking to Thea was like having a direct broadcast to the entire town.

Lake Basilites loved good Italian cuisine and equally delicious rumors and secrets to digest, and Thea was the purveyor of many secrets and the frequenter of my restaurant.

I kept my tablet out on the counter at the hostess station, smiling to myself at the gossip and the reactions of the townsfolk.

Thea cleared her throat and lifted a fork, the tines piercing a slice of thyme-infused mushroom and a perfectly al dente piece of farfalle pasta. "Seriously," she said, toying with her gold necklace, "can you believe that those goons ever thought they could compete with a place like this?"

I chewed on my bottom lip to stop from reacting.

First, my chef, Jacob, who happened to be my live-in boyfriend, would love the feedback that the customers were enjoying his newest creation.

Second, I despised the Morettis about as much as everyone else in town.

I'd never thought I'd have such a strong reaction to the family when they'd first arrived, but after the passing of their daughter, Lucia, at the end of summer, and the shuttering of their restaurant's doors, I was sad. A part of me was relieved—not because of

Lucia's death but because of the closing of the restaurant.

The Morettis felt *almost* like a problem of the past. Romeo was still at large, making a nuisance of himself, but that was manageable.

"You know, it serves them right for everything they've done," Thea continued, after finishing her bite of food. The other women paid rapt attention, fluttering eyelashes or leaning their elbows on the table to listen in.

"What do you mean, T?" Betty, another of Aunt Sof's gossipy friends, gave Thea a wide-eyed look. "They were a nuisance, but they haven't *done* anything that bad, right?"

"That's what you think," Thea said, setting her fork down.

My aunt had opted not to join in on this lunch gossip session—she had an appointment at the nail salon and then a big date with my Uncle Rocco tonight.

"Go on then," Amelda said, rolling sparkling emerald eyes heavenward. She was the most impatient of the group —antsy all the way up until they received their drinks order. A tall glass of white wine was her "poison of choice," as she called it. "Tell us the big secret. What is it that the Morettis have done that we don't know about?"

"It's not so much the Morettis as a family," Thea said, making sure she had every eye in the restaurant on her. She took another forkful of her pasta and chewed leisurely.

"The family is trouble, trouble and a pain in the neck, but there's more to it than that."

Was it just me, or did Thea look nervous?

Like she regretted saying anything?

Two pink spots had appeared in her cheeks as she sat back in her chair, glancing around the room at the other tables, clad with white tablecloths and decorated with crystal ware and the finest silver I could find in this small town.

"What's with you?" Amelda asked.

"Nothing," Thea said. "Just some things are better left as secrets."

"She's shvitzing," Betty said, leaning over and pressing the back of her hand, liver-spotted with age, to Thea's forehead. "She's practically got a fever over here."

Thea batted her friend's hand away. "I'm not. Just there are... Look, we can talk about it later. In a private place."

The other women at the table exchanged glances fraught with urgency and excitement. What was it that Thea was keeping a secret? And why?

I let out a sigh and turned my attention back to my tablet. I was organizing the tables for the day. A few customers had called in and canceled their reservations, which wasn't ideal during this time of the year.

We'd just come out of summer, which meant that

there were fewer tourists to pad the seats and the bank account of the restaurant. But now that we were the only Italian restaurant in Lake Basil, I wasn't too concerned about it.

The numbers looked good. And that was a relief after years of struggle.

But I couldn't afford to be lax.

Still, my mind wandered and my gaze with it. Dingle's Bakery across the street was doing a fantastic trade, and after my shift today, I got to pick up my best friend and head out to the house. We'd planned on taking a break together, lounging around at the lake house, making a fire and eating some s'mores.

Matilda, Jumbo, and I rarely got to hang out because of our busy schedules.

"—Romeo Moretti," Betty said.

"I heard that too," Amelda put in.

For once, Thea didn't say anything in response.

I frowned, lifting my head to scan the table. All their drinks were topped up, and their food wasn't done yet, but these women preferred to eat slowly and gossip for most of the meal, so that was normal.

Why was Thea acting different all of a sudden?

Her dark eyes kept flickering to the left, her attention moving toward the back of the restaurant, and I followed that gaze.

There was nothing there except the cozy brick wall, the painting that had been put up of Uncle Rocco, Aunt Sofia, and a pre-teen me. My arms were around Uncle Rocco's waist as we stood in front of what had been Romano's Pizza Parlor.

But that couldn't be what had Thea's attention, so what was it?

"Man's a real lothario, if you ask me," Betty said. "He's been flitting around town, flirting with every woman in sight."

"Wouldn't be surprised by that. He's not a bad-looking guy."

"Women are a sucker for a man in—"

Thea rose from her seat abruptly. "I'm feeling ill," she said.

The other women at her table cooed and expressed concern. "What's wrong, Thea, honey?" Amelda asked, rising as well. "Do you want me to drive you home?"

"No," Thea said. "No, I'm good. Just need some extra rest. Didn't sleep so well last night." And then she opened her purse and removed a few notes from it. She placed them on the table. "Let me know if I owe extra. I gotta go." She tucked her purse over her arm and rushed out of the glass front door.

Thea stumbled a step, then continued down the street.

Concern bubbled through my belly.

"What was that about?" Betty asked. "She's never that jumpy."

"Bet it's got something to do with those Morettis. You saw the way she acted after we started asking about her *secrets,*" Amelda said.

The other women nodded agreement.

"That's what happens when you keep secrets," Betty said ominously. "They come back to bite you where the sun don't shine."

"When you least expect it," Amelda agreed.

Two

I finally had my own car again, and it was amazing. To be fair, I missed my old car, particularly after everything I went through in it, but this was good. It was a fresh start.

"Such a smooth ride," Matilda said, looking back at Jumbo in his cat carrier on the back seat. "I can barely tell we're moving."

"That's because it's a hybrid," I said, patting the sleek dashboard proudly. "Electric and gas. Can you believe that? Fair enough, I don't know all the specs or whatever, but Jacob is great with cars. He said Lexus was the way to go. Reliable. Smooth ride. He said they're practically bulletproof."

Matilda wriggled her nose expressively, pressing her hand through her graying hair. "Wait, literally?"

"I wish," I said. "Not that I get shot at all that often."

Matilda pulled a face at that.

After the past couple of years we'd had, we couldn't say that Lake Basil was the safest place around. It seemed that every time we got rid of one treacherous murderer, another of the suckers popped up.

I felt like I was playing an illegal version of Whack-A-Mole. Illegal because I wasn't a cop.

But the past month had been quiet, and I'd had plenty of time to settle into the lake house with Jacob.

We parked outside, and Jumbo gave an insistent meow from the back seat.

"Almost, Jumbo," Matilda called back to him. "We're going to get you inside, and then you can have some water and snacks."

Jumbo gave a second meow, less insistent than the first, and Matilda grabbed the carrier from the back seat. I waited for her in front of my silver beast of a car, admiring its lines and the front grille.

A brisk fall breeze whipped around my shoulders, tugging at the neat jacket I'd chosen to pair with my blouse and suit pants for the day. Matilda came over, my polar opposite in a pastel shirt and a pair of faded blue jeans, one lock escaping from her bun. "There," she said. "Ready to go."

Jumbo hooked a white paw through the carrier door and meowed again.

"All right, all—" I paused, stopping at the front door of Jacob's gorgeous lake home.

"Gina? What is it?"

I bent and swept up a red rose from the welcome mat that Jacob and I had picked out together a couple of weeks ago.

"Aw, that's sweet," Matilda said, while Jumbo worried the front grate of his kitty carrier. "Jacob's so romantic."

I shook my head. "It's not Jacob," I said. "It's Shawn. I think."

"Huh?"

"Let's go inside and I'll fill you in." I let us into the lake house, and I inhaled the fresh scent of the cookies Jacob had baked yesterday, as well as the smell of wood polish and a hint of lemon. The house always smelled the same, lived in and happy, and with a hint of whatever Jacob had made the day before.

I checked the front door was locked, a thread of alarm traveling through my body.

Was it silly to be afraid of getting roses?

Shawn was pushing his luck by doing this.

Matilda bent and let Jumbo out of the carrier, then made quick work of pouring him a bowl of water and one of the food from the kitty supply bag she'd brought with her. Jumbo stretched and purred, meowing at us with his tail shaking.

I stroked him, frowning, the rose in one hand.

"So, what's going on? Why is Shawn sending you roses?" Matilda asked.

I beckoned for her to follow me through to the kitchen, where I unceremoniously dumped the rose in the trash. "I don't know," I said.

"You don't?"

"No. You know that Shawn confessed his feelings to me a while ago," I said.

Matilda nodded. I told her everything because she was the best friend I'd ever had. "Sure. But I thought you gave him a clear picture about it never being a thing."

"I did. I told him that I'd chosen Jacob. For heaven's sake, I've moved in with Jacob. We're in love. It's not like I've ever led Shawn on to believe that we could ever be a thing," I said. "But he keeps on trying, and it's kind of bothering me now."

"Does Jacob know?" Matilda asked.

"No," I said. "I don't want to worry him."

A silence followed, and I took the moment to start preparing coffee for us. Matilda liked her tea, but coffee was a treat she enjoyed whenever we were together. I made her one, using the barista quality coffee machine that Jacob and I shared.

Another new addition.

We'd decided that if there was one thing we weren't going to skimp on in our home, it was coffee. We were both unabashed addicts.

Matilda sat down at the cozy kitchen table, the one where we'd shared many a family dinner with Uncle Rocco and Aunt Sofia, and tapped her trimmed nails on the wood. *Tappity-tap. Tappity-tap.*

"What?" I asked, setting a cappuccino in front of her and starting on mine.

Matilda drew in a mouthful of coffee and studied me over the rim of her mug with those sparkling blue eyes that saw far too much. Jumbo wandered into the kitchen and sat near the fridge, licking his white paws enthusiastically. He always ate in record time.

"What?" I repeated.

"Why haven't you told Jacob?"

"Like I said, I don't want to worry him."

"Gina."

"What? I'm serious. Jacob *really* doesn't like Shawn. Like at all," I said. "The last time they saw each other, they almost had a fight. The last thing I need is their beef to affect our relationship or the restaurant."

"How might that happen?" Matilda asked.

"Think about it," I said. "Shawn is the detective. He might

not be the sheriff, but he still has authority in this town. And it's not like Sheriff Stills likes my family. The last thing I need is Jacob fighting with Shawn and then it affecting the business."

"Those," Matilda said, putting down her mug, "are some solid mental gymnastics you're doing."

"Hey!"

"You're afraid to tell your loyal, loving, live-in boyfriend—"

"Nice alliteration."

"—that the weird detective who has a crush on you is making you uncomfortable and leaving flowers at your shared home because you think he will lose his temper and attack said stalker detective?"

"Yeah."

Matilda shook her head. "That doesn't sound like a very Jacob thing to do. The man's rational."

Jumbo meowed.

"Don't gang up on me." I pointed a finger at Matilda and then at the cat, who ignored me and kept on cleaning himself.

"I don't think you need to hide this, Gina," Matilda said. "I think you should tell Jacob that the problem with Shawn hasn't gone away, and then I think you should tell Shawn that you don't appreciate him leaving you flowers. The truth will set you free."

"That's the thing," I said. "I'm not sure about... This sounds silly, but what if I'm wrong?"

"About what?"

"About the flowers being from Shawn?" I asked. "What if it's someone else leaving me roses?"

"You are a gorgeous, successful woman, so that's entirely possible," Matilda said with a smile.

"Not what I meant. What if it's someone bad?" My heart thrummed against the inside of my chest. The words that I'd been holding back over the past couple of weeks were finally free to the world. "What if it's someone who's mad at me for all the trouble I've been causing?"

"And by trouble, you mean keeping the town safe from murderers and wannabe mobsters?" Matilda narrowed one eye behind her glasses.

"Yeah," I said.

"Look, if that's the case, that's even *more* reason to tell Jacob. And to go to the cops about it," Matilda said.

She had a point.

But my stomach tensed. Something *strange* was going on in Lake Basil this fall. I wanted to know what it was.

Three

The following morning...

JACOB HAD WORKED LATE AT THE RESTAURANT last night, and it had been one of my only nights off. Unsurprisingly, I'd spent a lot of my evening pondering the roses and what Matilda had said the previous afternoon.

While I was all for honesty and truth and secrets being out in the open, I had a resistance to telling Jacob about the roses.

To me, it seemed more logical to talk to Shawn first, get him to stop leaving roses on my doorstep, and then let bygones be bygones. Fewer issues caused, no room for conflict and trouble that neither of us needed in our lives.

Jacob and I were happy, and I didn't want anything to

ruin that after what we'd been through as a couple—mostly on account of my drama.

And if it wasn't Shawn sending the roses…?

I should talk to Aunt Sof. She'd know who might be doing this if it isn't *Shawn.*

What sense did it make for Shawn to send me roses after I'd told him I was happy with Jacob?

I sat in my favorite spot at the table in the backyard, wrapped up tight in my fluffy PJ robe, the morning chill brushing against my cheeks. It wasn't cold enough to stay inside, particularly since Jacob had set up a fire for us in a portable fire pit.

He was inside right now, brewing up another pot of coffee and fixing us breakfast.

The house still needed some work, but piece by piece, we'd started fixing it up. New paint here, sanding down the wood there, fixing broken pieces, and the next step would be talking to contractors.

Jacob's phone lit up on the outdoor table, and I glanced over, catching a glimpse of the notification.

It was a reminder that flashed across the screen.

Go to jewelry store and check out rings.

My heart froze in my chest, and I forgot to breathe.

I reached out a hand, considering picking up his phone, then shook my head. It wasn't my place to meddle in Jacob's affairs. Privacy was a big deal to me. At least when it came to people who weren't murder suspects.

Rings. He's looking at rings.

The screen door clapped behind me before I could think too much about it, and Jacob's footsteps crunched through the grass.

"Here you go," Jacob said. He planted a kiss on my cheek and placed a plate of Eggs Benedict in front of me.

"You really should let me do more of the cooking," I said. "I can barely handle the guilt of having delicious meals cooked for me every day when you spend the rest of *your* day cooking in the kitchen at the restaurant."

"Cooking is one of my favorite things to do," Jacob said. "Apart from spending time with you."

My heart fluttered, and the nerves at what I'd seen on his phone increased. I opened my mouth to say something, then thought better of it. Jacob knew I wasn't quite ready to get married yet.

But it wasn't a bad thing that he was thinking about the future. Our future.

I cut into the eggs and found them just the right amount of runny. I lifted a piece to my mouth, but a flicker of movement caught my eye.

The black cat that had been frequenting our home, occasionally breaking in, or meowing at our windows late at night, stalked through the bushes near the back door.

"There he is," I whispered, putting down my fork. "See?"

Jacob turned his head. "Poor thing. He's so skinny."

"They say you shouldn't feed stray cats, but it's clear that he doesn't have an owner, Jacob." For the longest time, we'd thought the cat belonged to a neighbor, but the more it came around the more clear it became that wasn't the case.

"That's it," Jacob said. "I'm going to stop by the pet store on my way to work and grab some cat food and a couple bowls."

"That's a great idea," I said. "Maybe a nice warm kitty bed, too."

"So, now he's moving in?" Jacob asked, the corner of his lip lifting. "Just like that?"

I laughed. "I don't see why not. He needs a home, Jake, and we've got a great one."

He gave me a soft look, reached out and touched a hand to my cheek. "I love when—"

A loud croak interrupted him, and we both froze.

"What on earth was—?"

A spatter of green-black dropped from the tree over our heads and landed slap in the middle of my plate. I let out a yell and nearly fell out of my chair.

Jacob leaped up to help me.

We both craned our necks, peering into the tree.

Far above us, a large black crow sat on a branch. It cocked its dark head to one side, studying us with a beady black eye that could only be considered malevolent.

I was a lover of most animals—barring insects—but even I could tell this crow didn't have the best of intentions. Maybe that was because he'd pooped all over my breakfast before I could even grab a bite of it.

"Hey," Jacob said. "Shoo."

"Shoo," the crow replied.

We both stared in a mixture of awe and horror.

"Jake. Jake, did that crow just—"

"I believe it just shooed us," Jacob said. "Verbally."

"Shoo," the crow repeated.

"Crows can talk?" I asked.

"Learn something new every day," Jacob said. "Someone must have taught it how to say—"

"Shoo, you poo!" the crow croaked, the black feathers at its throat lifting and settling as it talked. "Shoo, you poo! This is my house! This is my house!"

"Well, OK," I said. "I guess we should be grateful nobody taught it how to cuss." This was Lake Basil, after all.

"Shoo, you poo!"

"What do we do?" I asked. "Should we chase it away? It might be somebody's pet."

Before Jacob could answer, the crow took flight,

spreading its massive black wings and sweeping out of the tree. I ducked, lifting my arms, but the crow wasn't interested in me. Instead, it took aim at the cat, diving toward it.

"Hey!" I darted across the yard. "Hey, you leave him alone!" I waved my arms, and the crow changed course, flying off over our house and out of sight. The black cat had already disappeared, spooked by my show of anti-crow aggression.

What the heck was going on in Lake Basil?

Four

My Aunt Sofia preened and plumped her hair in the front hall, the house phone receiver pinned to her ear. She held the door open with her foot to let me into the cramped hall of my childhood home. She blew me a kiss, and I leaned in and hugged her, catching an earful of the gossipy conversation on the other end of the phone.

My aunt was shorter than me, but we had the same dark curly hair. The similarities between us ended there, but that was what I loved about my aunt. She was completely different from me, and a wonderful person.

"Don't tell me he's been giving you trouble again," Aunt Sof said to her friend on the phone. I shut the door, and she covered the receiver. "Be with you in a sec. Rocco's at the store. Coffee and cookies in the kitchen."

I grinned at that, and made my way past her and into

the cozy kitchen where a plate of chocolate chip cookies waited on the table, and the coffee pot was just done brewing. I poured two mugs of coffee then sat down to wait.

"No!" Aunt Sof cried. "No, you're kidding me. He said that? And then what did *she* say?"

A silence.

A gasp.

"You're kidding. Like that? That's so far out of line, the lines are not even a thing anymore," she said. "Right? I know, right?"

Oh boy. This might take a while.

I took a bite of a cookie, enjoying the crunchy goodness but frowning. I'd found another rose on the doorstep this morning. I'd found it just as we were about to leave, and I'd tossed it aside into the bushes before Jacob could see it.

It felt icky to hide it from him, but I really had to figure out whether these roses were threatening or not. If they were from Shawn, it was an easy fix. If they were from a stalker, then I would let Jacob know.

No need to freak him out.

Mental gymnastics. The words floated through my mind in Matilda's voice.

Finally, Aunt Sofia entered the kitchen and lowered herself into the seat across from mine. She was always neat, in the way she ate and moved, and this morning was no exception. She picked up her cookie, took a bite, and then dusted off her fingers over the plate. "Gina, I've missed you. You don't visit enough now that you've gotten yourself a man." I knew Aunt Sofia wasn't serious.

If she'd been serious, she wouldn't have said it at all. She preferred to avoid difficult conversations rather than meet them head on.

"Missed you too," I said, and finished the last of my cookie, sweeping the crumbs off the table. "These are amazing, by the way."

"Take some home for Jacob," Aunt Sof said. "I've got so many, they're practically comin' out of my ears. Besides, if you don't take 'em, Rocky will eat them and the doctor's going to get angry with me."

Uncle Rocco was meant to limit the sweet stuff and watch his weight. He was at risk of high blood pressure and had been on a diet for a while now. Any time Aunt Sof had to make cookies for a friend, a bake sale, or her book club, we had to eat them or hide them before he could find them.

When it came to food, my uncle was a man on a mission.

Not that I blamed him. I was a food lover myself.

"How are you, Auntie?" I asked. "I saw your friends at the restaurant the other day. Thea was her usual gossipy self." Apart from when she'd run out of the restaurant claiming to be ill.

"I was just talking to Betty about her earlier. She's been acting real weird lately, and nobody can figure out why. Keeps saying she feels sick. I'd say she was pregnant if she wasn't past the age where she can get pregnant, you know?"

"Auntie."

"And she's single. But that never stopped a determined—"

"All right," I said, before she could gather too much gossip steam. "I had a question for you."

"Oh, well, fire away, sweetheart."

I took a sip of my coffee, inhaled through my nose, and then told my aunt everything about the roses. "So, I have my suspicions that it's either Shawn, or it's someone more sinister."

"S-Sinister," Aunt Sofia murmured, touching her fingers to her lips. "Surely not."

"I don't know what to think," I said.

Aunt Sofia pressed her lips together and released them. "Well, you're probably right not to worry Jacob about this until you're sure. And I think I know how I can help you."

"How?"

"If anyone's going to know who might be leaving roses on doorsteps in Lake Basil, it's Thea." Aunt Sofia frowned.

"In fact, I heard a rumor that there's been a lot of unrequited love and romance floating around town. People doing things they shouldn't be doing. I'll talk to her about it."

"Really? You think Thea can help?"

"Yes," Aunt Sofia said firmly. "Without a doubt. The woman knows everybody's business, whether they like it or not."

"I'm not sure how to feel about that," I said.

"As long as you have nothing to hide," Aunt Sofia said, "you should feel fine."

I laughed, and Aunt Sofia took another cookie off the plate and bit into it. "I'll give her a call and see what she has to say. Wait right here."

"What, right now?"

"Sure! Unless you need to get to the restaurant?"

"I do, but I can wait a minute."

Aunt Sofia rewarded me with a smile and scooted off her chair. She hurried out into the hall and left me in the kitchen to eat cookies, sip coffee, and considered what Aunt Sofia had said. How on earth could Thea help me?

A couple of minutes later, Aunt Sofia returned to the kitchen, frowning deeply.

"Aunt Sof?"

"She's not picking up her phone," she said. "I called her house phone and her cell phone and she's not answering either. She's not the type of person who does that."

"Huh. Are you sure she's not in the bathroom or something? She did say she felt ill."

"Yeah. Yeah, I guess, but it's strange, Gina," Aunt Sofia said. "I don't know if it's because you mentioned sinister people or if something's really wrong, but I've got a bad feelin' about it."

"Where does she stay?" I asked. "I can stop by and check on her for you."

"You would do that?"

"Of course, Auntie. If you're worried, I—"

The phone rang and Aunt Sofia rushed out to answer it. "Oh, Thea. You scared me! I thought something had happened to you."

I let out the breath I'd been holding. Thea was fine. But it was sweet that Aunt Sofia had been that worried about her friend, even if it was paranoid.

Was it paranoid in this town? There had been too many murders in Lake Basil, and we didn't need another one.

$$Five$$

The following morning...

THANKFULLY, THERE HADN'T BEEN ANY ROSES left out for me overnight. Jacob had already darted off to work to start training a new chef we'd hired, and I had the house to myself for a few hours.

I made myself a cup of coffee with our fancy machine, then walked through to the living room and stared out at the lake, taking occasional sips and feeling grateful for the robe and the indoor heating now that fall was starting to get seriously nippy.

The black cat from yesterday hadn't made its reappearance, but neither had the crow—a good sign. I didn't know what it meant that a crow had pooped in my breakfast, but I'd wager it wasn't a great portent for the future.

I took a sip of my coffee and paused, frowning at the lake.

At this time of the morning, most folks had already zipped off to work, and the lake would be quiet—especially since tourist season was all but over in Lake Basil.

But there was a crowd on the shore opposite in front of the Lake Basil Guesthouse.

I set my coffee down on the coffee table and moved toward the windows to get a better look.

"What the—?"

There weren't just a few people, either. It was an entire crowd, and they were gathered around one person in particular.

What was that about?

A flash of blue lights parted the group, and my heart leaped into my throat. Something serious. Bad, even.

I had to know what it was.

I changed out of my PJs, brushed my teeth, and rushed out to my new Lexus. Within fifteen minutes, I was circling the lake, bumping over the dirt road that would never be fixed. It was a feature of the town.

I parked outside the guesthouse further back from the tree with its tire swing, and got out.

Several screens had been erected on the lake shore and police officers were rolling out a crime scene tape. I scanned the gathered officials, but Detective Carter was nowhere to be seen.

A crowd stood on the steps and porch of the guesthouse, murmuring amongst themselves. I hurried up to them, making sure to give the officers and crime scene a wide berth. The last thing I needed was *more* trouble with the law.

I'd had enough of that, and of murderers, to last me a lifetime.

Don't get your hopes up.

I stopped beside Sasha, a librarian with cornrows, yellow-framed glasses, and a wicked sense of humor. "Hey, Sasha," I said.

She drew me into a hug. "Gina. There you are. Wondered when we'd be seeing you here."

"Huh?"

"Oh, honey, come on," she said. "We all know that whenever a body turns up, you're bound to follow a couple of minutes later."

"Sometimes even before," Lou added in—he worked at the antique store and loved gossiping, silk ascots, and took his ravioli with extra parmesan.

It was nice to see two friendly faces, regulars of the restaurant now, and I let out a breath to ease the tension that had built inside me. "A body," I said. "Seriously?"

"A body," Lou said conspiratorially. "And that's not even the worst part. It's a murder."

Sasha shuddered and rubbed her arms, her bracelets clinking together delicately. "Again," she said. "Can you believe it? Again?"

"I *can* believe it," Lou said. "I mean, look at what's been happening over the past couple of months. It's a miracle the FBI haven't descended on this town. I'm starting to think there's some type of bad energy that's taken over here."

Sasha rolled her eyes. "You and the energy."

"Murder," I said, stroking my chin. "Did you see anything interesting?"

Lou and Sasha exchanged a glance. "Did we ever," Lou said, wriggling a plucked eyebrow. He was always so well put together, I envied him. "Detective Shawn took Romeo Moretti inside to talk to him."

"Rumor has it, he was found standing over the body," Sasha added in. "But I don't believe it for a second."

"Of course you don't," Lou said. "You're practically Romeo's shadow at this point."

"I am not."

"We both know why you wanted me to come have breakfast at the guesthouse this morning.

I tuned out the argument and focused on the important part—that Romeo had been found standing over a dead body.

Not this again. It seemed like the Morettis were *always* involved in the shenanigans around town. And I had been suspicious of Romeo for a while, but he'd never been the murderer. That didn't mean he wasn't capable though.

And to be found standing over a dead body?

This wasn't like the last time when I'd merely suspected it because he'd been in the general area. This was him, caught standing over a corpse.

"She's got that look on her face again," Lou said, with a twinkle in his eye.

"That's not the only thing," Sasha said. "Apparently, the victim was stabbed."

"Did you see the body?" I asked.

"No, but Beau got an eyeful of it, and he's talking to another officer right now. He was pretty upset about it. Poor Beau's been through enough after what happened the last time."

I nodded then sighed. "Yeah." Beau was the owner of the guesthouse and an all-round nice guy. He was respected in Lake Basil and for a good reason. The guesthouse had always been neutral ground, no matter who was arguing with whom.

Uncle Rocco had once told me that he'd met up with the sheriff here to discuss their disagreements. It had almost come to blows but Beau had brought them under control with hot chocolate and calm words.

The poor guy didn't need the added stress.

"Do we know who the victim is?" I asked.

"That's the worst part," Sasha said.

Lou lowered his head, shaking it and sniffing loudly. He reached into the pocket of his jeans and withdrew a pack of Kleenex, extracting a tissue so that he could dab underneath either eye.

"It's Thea."

My eyes widened, and a ringing started up in my ears. Thea?

"Thea?"

"Thea," Sasha confirmed. "Thea Wakefield."

"That's—Oh, that's so terrible." I couldn't find the right words. When my aunt found out about this, she was going to be devastated, especially after she'd been so concerned yesterday. *She was onto something.*

Aunt Sof had told me that Thea wasn't acting like her normal self, and I should have listened. I should have realized that something wasn't right.

I let out a low breath. "This is bad."

"Thea was a pillar of this community," Lou said, between sniffs and dabs. "I can't believe she's gone."

"I don't think it's properly registered yet," Sasha said. "The last time I saw her she seemed so happy. Just yesterday, at the post office. She was there collecting a package, and she was fine."

"Fine? Happy? You're sure?" I asked. "She wasn't acting strange?"

"It depends on what you consider 'strange'." Sasha shrugged. "She was whistling when she left the post office, but when I asked her about the package, she was jumpy. Yeah. And when she started off down the street, she kind of looked both ways first."

"You're supposed to do that," Lou said, then blew his nose loudly.

"That's when you cross the street." Sasha tapped him on the shoulder. "I mean she looked up and down the street before she walked off. Like she was looking for some-one. Or expecting someone to be there. She sort of scanned everywhere—up, down, all around, and then walked off."

I tapped my chin, but before I could say anything, a door banged behind us.

Six

ROMEO MORETTI STRODE OUT ONTO THE PORCH, shrugging on his leather jacket. He swept a hand over his parted hair then gave me a look. One eye narrowed, the corner of his lip twisting upward in disdain.

The guests and intrigued onlookers quieted at his presence.

It said something that he wasn't in cuffs. That he hadn't been taken down to the station. And I didn't see blood spatter on his clothes. But it was possible that he'd worn protective clothing that he'd discarded before the cops got here.

"What are you looking at?" Romeo asked, making eye contact with me and then a few others. Moretti wasn't the type of guy to shut up when he was under pressure. No, he preferred to go on the attack.

Romeo met my gaze as he took a cigarette out of his jacket pocket, followed it with a lighter. He flipped the lid open, lit the end of his cigarette then crooked a finger in my direction before walking off the porch.

Lou let out a low whistle. "Say what you want about the man, he's got that *thing* about him doesn't he?"

"A real bad boy," Sasha murmured.

I frowned.

What was Moretti playing at? Beckoning me like I would come when he called?

The man strode across the neatly trimmed lawn and stopped next to my car. He leaned against the Lexus and tilted his head, watching the officers and the screens that blocked the crime scene from view.

I said goodbye to Sasha and Lou and then headed down to meet him.

"How did you know this was my car?" I asked Romeo.

"Make it my business to know things."

He wasn't the only one. Thea had made it her business to know things, and she'd wound up on the lake shore.

"Get off, would you?" I shooed him before he scratched the paint.

Romeo smirked at me but did as I'd asked. He finished his cigarette and stubbed it out underfoot. "Give me a ride?"

"Why would I do that, Moretti? We're not exactly best friends."

"You solved my sister's murder case," he said. "I don't like you, but I trust you more than I trust any of these other goons." He pointed to the police. "Especially the ones in blue."

I studied him. "But *I* don't trust *you*."

"Your loss," he said. "Could've told you what I saw." Romeo gave me a challenging stare. "But I guess you're not interested in solving mysteries anymore, huh?"

I glared back at him. "Get in the car. No smoking." I opened my door and let him in.

Romeo got into my Lexus and made himself comfortable. "Take me back to my place," he said.

I hated the way he demanded things, but if I wanted information then I'd have to take it as it came. I started my car and drove off, unconcerned about what the people on the porch might think about this. Lou and Sasha knew the deal.

We drove in silence for a couple of minutes until we parked outside the Moretti mansion's fabulous gates.

"Well?" I prompted.

Romeo sniffed. "It was the guesthouse owner who offed her."

"Beau?"

"That's right," he said. "I was following her this morning, early, just before the sun came up. Stopped outside the guest house. It was dark. Couldn't see her, but I heard him attack her."

"You heard him? How did you know it was him?" I was highly skeptical of this. First, I didn't entirely trust Moretti, and second, why would Beau have killed Thea? He was a peaceful guy. Not the kind of person who attacked others, and he'd been friends with Thea, hadn't he? He was friends with everyone.

Romeo took his time answering. He checked his phone then sighed. "Cos I heard her greet him," he said.

"By name?"

"No. But after she was stabbed, I stepped out, and I saw him standing on the porch."

"Wait, so she was stabbed on the lake shore, yet when you stepped out he was on the guesthouse porch?"

"Yeah. Then he decided to accuse me and call the cops," Romeo said.

"That doesn't add up, Moretti," I said. "How did he get back onto the porch so soon after stabbing her?" Allegedly.

"I don't know. Didn't say I have all the answers, did I?" Romeo tucked his phone away. "But it was him. He's the guy I'd check out if I were you." His hand moved to the door handle.

"Wait," I said. "Is that it? Isn't there anything else that happened? Anything relevant?"

Romeo shrugged.

"Why were you following Thea in the first place?"

His lips thinned.

"Moretti."

"None of your business."

"You were the one who said you'd tell me—"

"I wanted a ride," he said, and clunked my car door open. He started getting out, but I caught the sleeve of his jacket and tugged on it. Romeo yanked it free and clicked his fingers at me. "Don't touch me, woman. You'll regret it."

"Just like Thea did?"

"Now, you listen to me, I didn't do nothing to her. I'm not that dumb," he said. "It was the guesthouse owner. Got it?"

I gritted my teeth. "Romeo," I said, "you've got to give me more to go on than that." Man, I didn't like this guy, but I needed him to give me as much as he had if I wanted to figure out what had happened to my aunt's friend. "The cops are going to be all over you like parmigiana on a wheel, so if you want to keep operating how you like to operate, you've got to make it easy on me."

Romeo's lip curled in disgust. "There was a rose."

"What?"

"She was holding a rose," he said. "I saw her walking along with a rose, heading over to the guesthouse just before the sun rose. I followed her all the way there. She kept looking around like she expected someone was following her, so I had to hide behind a tree. That's when I heard the attack."

"Why didn't you jump out? Help her?"

"I didn't realize what it was until after it had happened," he said.

"What color was the rose?"

"Red. Saw it after she was stabbed," he said. "Well, if it wasn't red before, it sure would've been red after. Thanks for the ride, sugar." And then strolled up to the gates. They opened for him and he entered, swaggering off like he owned Lake Basil.

I let out a breath, despising that the interior of my car smelled of his expensive cologne. I opened the windows and put it in reverse, then got out of there, taking the slow drive back to the house so that I could freshen up and prepare for the day.

But I was, as the kids would say, "shooketh."

Thea was dead. Stabbed. Romeo was involved yet again, and poor Beau was being accused even though he was the least likely suspect I'd ever encountered. The man was Lake Basil's guardian angel. Besides that, my aunt would soon find out—I'd call her first to break the news so that she wouldn't hear it through the grapevine—and there had been a rose on her dead body.

A rose.

Surely that didn't mean what I thought it meant.

Surely the rose was a coincidence.

Seven

THE RESTAURANT HAD ONLY JUST OPENED FOR lunch and was already packed with diners. Whenever a traumatic or interesting event took place in Lake Basil, the residents had to talk about it and they had to eat. The two went hand-in-hand in this town. And it helped that there was a sense of family in our restaurant.

People felt safe at Romano's, they felt the love in the food, and the joy that came with being part of an Italian family like mine. I relished that on most days, but today, I would've given anything for the restaurant to quiet down a little so I could think.

Vi and Charles were swept off their feet with the tables, so much so that I'd pulled our new server in for an emergency shift. The kitchen was producing dishes as fast as it could, and I'd taken up the cheese to circle through the restaurant and offer extra to those who needed it, grater at the ready.

"Can't believe it—"

"—such a huge loss."

"I don't understand how this could have happened."

"—Romeo Moretti."

"Beau? You're out of your mind."

"Mad dumb. Romeo—"

I picked up snippets of conversations as I moved through the space. The hum of chatter was so loud that it overpowered the pleasant music tinkling from the speakers. Once I was sure everybody had the right amount of parmesan cheese, I returned to the hostess station to check on our lunch reservations. We were full up, but the current tables should empty out soon enough to make room for—

The front door opened, and the diners went quiet.

Shawn Carter, the broad-shouldered, balding detective, entered the restaurant. My insides squirmed and squeezed.

It was the first time I'd come face-to-face with Shawn since he'd started leaving roses on my doorstep, and I was *so* not ready for this confrontation. I didn't want to talk to him about it now.

If it was him and not the murderer.

Why else would Thea have had a rose in her hand? Unless she'd found it? Or was it just a coincidence? I wasn't a gardening expert, but I had noticed that there was a second bloom in fall in Lake Basil, when the cooler temperatures started setting in.

Shawn nodded toward a few of the regulars at their tables, and the volume in the restaurant increased again as people picked up their conversations. Most wouldn't care if Shawn overheard them gossiping—this was Lake Basil and people talked.

"Good afternoon, Shawn," I said, as politely as I could manage. It was silly, but I felt a lot of anger toward him for not taking my hint. I wasn't interested romantically. It was not OK that he'd decided to press the issue. "We're fully booked for lunch, but I can slot you in for an early dinner."

"Gina," he said, and he looked paler than usual. Was it just me or was he sweating? He ran his hand over his brow, rearranged the lanyard that hung against his neatly buttoned shirt. "Gina, we need to talk."

I opened my mouth then shut it again.

The temptation to find out more about the murder investigation was almost overwhelming, but I didn't want to, yet again, give Shawn the wrong idea. I didn't need him leaving me chocolates or teddy bears next. "Is this a personal or professional matter, Shawn?" I asked. "Because we're swamped, and I've got duties to attend to."

Shawn's gaze swept over the restaurant.

"It's a professional matter," he said. "Step outside with me, will you?"

The sky had started to bruise, bringing with it the promise of rain, but the first droplets had yet to fall. "How long is this going to take?" I asked.

It occurred to me then that I was hesitating because I didn't feel safe with Shawn anymore. He had pressed the boundaries of our friendship too far. Then again, I had done the same, except in a "professional" capacity by interfering in unsolved crimes.

"Not long enough that things will get out of control in here," Shawn said. "Look, it will take a couple of minutes at best. Just come outside with me."

I begrudgingly set my tablet down and followed him, tucking my suit jacket close to my body. "What's going on?" I asked.

"I think you know what's going on, Gina," he said.

"I assume you're talking about what happened to Thea."

Shawn paled even further, though it didn't seem possible, and he rolled his lips together. A wind swept past us, tugging at his shirt and lifting the fine ginger hairs on his head. "Yeah."

"Are you OK? You look kind of pale and sickly."

"Gee thanks."

"You know what I mean, Shawn. You need to sit down

or something?"

"I'm good," he said, waving away my concern. "Look, I don't want to do this anymore than you want to, but we gotta talk about what happened."

Roses? Murder? "Huh?"

"Thea's dead," he said. "She's been stabbed. Romeo was found standing over her body."

"Right?"

"And the first thing you do is drive up to the crime scene, start asking questions, and then proceed to get into a car with the prime suspect and drive off."

He'd seen that. Just my luck. "I was giving a friend a ride," I said.

"That's a lie and we both know it. You and Moretti are about as agreeable with each other as a lion and a hyena fighting over a dead animal."

I frowned. "Who's the hyena in this scenario?" Better yet. "Who's the dead animal?"

Another wave of his hand. "Look," he said, "look, I'm just saying that this isn't gonna fly. This habit of yours to interfere in everything we do at the police station... Look, Sheriff Stills is starting to reach the end of his rope."

"Yeah?" I couldn't say that I cared. The sheriff had messed with my aunt and uncle one too many times.

"Yeah. So this time, I'm gonna need you to stay the heck out of it, Gina."

"Or what?" The words were out of me before I could stop them. I didn't like threats. And I was annoyed with Shawn already.

"Or I'll make you," he said.

"What's that supposed to mean?"

He took a step toward me.

"Look, Gina, you know I want what's best for you," he said, "but this has got to stop. If you set a foot wrong, I'll shut this place down."

"What place?"

"The restaurant."

"Are you kidding me?" I asked. "You're joking. You'll shut down my restaurant if I don't do as you say? I hate to break it to you, Shawn, but that's illegal. You can't do that."

"I could arrest you for obstructing," he said. "I could do any number of things."

"Power tripping. Or just trippin'."

Shawn grimaced, stroking his hand over his five o'clock shadow. "Look, I'm giving you fair warning. Don't mess with me this time around."

"Why? You never cared before?"

"Not up for debate. I have the power to do what needs to be done, got it? And I'll use all that power. I'll come down on you if you sniff around," he said. "So. Stay. Out. Of. It." And then he strode off down the street.

Eight

That weekend...

THE ENTIRE TOWN HAD SHUTTERED ITS DOORS for the Sunday memorial service that was being held at the local Catholic church. Thea had been devout, and while a lot of us were from different religions, we'd gathered regardless.

Because this was Thea. And in Lake Basil, nobody cared who you worshiped or loved, we cared for you just the same, because you were one of our own.

And Thea had been an integral part of our community. A friend, a confidant, and a good person, even if she did like a good helping of gossip with her farfalle.

I sat on the polished wooden pew with my aunt on my left and Jacob on my right. Jake leaned on his knees, his fingers interlaced and a look of intense concentration on his face. Aunt Sofia held a tissue to her nose, her shoulders rocking silently, her free hand in Uncle Rocco's.

"—would have wanted us to remember her at her best, doing what she loved," Betty said, from where she stood at the front of the church. "She would want us to eat and be merry, to gossip and enjoy ourselves."

A ripple of smiles moved through the mourners in the church, rueful and sad.

"Mostly, she would want us to know that she loved us. She loved the town. She wanted what was best for—"

A door slammed, and a few people cried out.

I turned around in the pew in time to spot the tail-end of a fancy shoe disappearing out the front of the church. Someone had left in a hurry. Who?

Betty cleared her throat, a frown turning her lips down at the corners. "So, we're all going to meet up in the town hall after this, as the mayor has graciously agreed that we can continue the service there. Drinks and food will be served."

We sang a hymn together, and Aunt Sofia put away her tissue, grabbing for my hand and squeezing tight. Afterward, we piled into the Lexus and took the drive over to the town hall together. It was quiet in the car, apart from the occasional cough from Uncle Rocco or a sigh from my aunt.

The town hall was full of people who had known Thea, and I scanned the gathering. Notable Shawn hadn't come to pay his respects.

Just thinking about him made my blood pressure rise. I hadn't had the chance to bring up roses during our last "interlude" and I was still so darn angry at him for the way he'd threatened my business.

"I'll get you some food, Sof," Uncle Rocco said, then gestured for Jacob to join him.

Jake kissed me on the cheek before joining my uncle over at the buffet table that held an assortment of food, much of it donated by Thea's friends and distant relatives —notably, none of them had been in town on the morning of her death.

I guided my aunt to a table near the doors and sat her down because she was starting to look green.

"Are you OK, Auntie?"

Aunt Sof shook her head. "I just can't believe it," she said. "Thea." Then she shook her head rapidly. "Who am I kidding? I can believe it."

"What do you mean?"

"You remember the other day, honey," she said. "I was sure that something was wrong. I had a feeling that something bad was about to happen to T, and I was right." She swallowed, turning bloodshot eyes toward me. "I talked to her every morning. Every single morning. Whether it was in the nail salon or at our book club or just on the phone. Not a day went by without a chat on the phone."

"I'm so sorry, Auntie." I looped my arm around her shoulders and pulled her into a hug. "I know this isn't easy. None of it is."

"It really *isn't.*"

A silence fell between us as we watched more mourners arrive and people circled through the town hall, talking, drinking and eating.

"I'm going to figure out who did this," I said softly. "Don't worry."

"Promise me you will," Aunt Sofia whispered.

She wasn't one to suggest I put myself in danger, but her tone was serious.

"I swear it," I said. "No matter what. I'll make sure that her killer is brought to justice."

Another quiet. Jacob and Uncle Rocco were still perusing the buffet table and had been waylaid by a few of my uncle's buddies.

"I don't trust that Shawn," Aunt Sofia said.

My head whipped around and I searched her face. "Why?" My aunt was a gossip, but I'd never heard her say anything negative about Shawn. About the sheriff, maybe, but never Shawn. She was always fair in her assessment of a situation. Unless family was involved, and then there was a little bias.

"I heard a rumor that he was acting very strange on the morning of the murder," my aunt said. "That he arrived at the scene faster than any of the other officers. And that he was pale and sweaty for a whole day afterward." She took a breath. "And then there's the fact that he gets twitchy whenever somebody mentions the murder. Something isn't right, Gina."

"I hear you." And I felt the same way. "I have to figure out where to start."

"Thea knew everybody. Everybody and their business."

"Do you know of anyone who might have had a bone to pick with her?" I needed to populate my suspect list. So far, I had Romeo Moretti, an accusation against Beau to check out, and, most alarming of all, a suspicion about the detective working the case.

Could Shawn have done something? *The rose.*

"Thea definitely had enemies," she said. "I'll try to draw up a list so that you have something to work from, but I can't think of them right off the top of my head. I mean, she complained plenty of times about a bunch of different people who were annoying her."

"Romeo one of them?"

"Of course," she said. "But he annoys everyone."

"And Beau?"

"Beau?" Aunt Sof's brows drew together. "I don't

think so. No, she liked Beau the same as everybody else. I don't see why he would have been her enemy."

"Did Thea ever run afoul of the law?"

Aunt Sofia didn't answer right away. "I—No, I don't think so. But Shawn..." She trailed off as Uncle Rocco and Jacob approached.

They delivered plates of food to us then headed off again to get drinks. The pair chatted amiably, and I couldn't help the warmth that spread through my chest. Jacob fit in with my family so well.

"I promise, Auntie, I'll figure this out." I drew the plate of finger foods toward myself and picked up a cheese puff. I didn't have the appetite for it, but I inserted it between my lips and chewed mechanically, my mind turning over facts.

Thea had acted strangely before her murder. She'd collected a package from the post office. Could that be a part of this?

She had been stabbed. Where was the murder weapon? Why had there been a rose on the scene? Why had Moretti been following her? Why was Beau on the porch? Why was Shawn acting strange and coming over pale and shaky whenever someone mentioned the murder?

Questions. So many questions.

The following day...

AUNT SOFIA'S LIST HAD BEEN NEARLY exhaustive. There were so many names on it, my eyes watered at the prospect of reading it in full, let alone visiting every person she'd listed. So, the morning after the memorial service, I gave Jacob a kiss on the cheek and headed into town alone to visit my best friend.

Matilda stood behind the counter in Dingle's Bakery, a smile on her lips, a cute cream and pink apron bearing the logo of her business on the front. It was past eight in the morning, but the bakery was bustled with customers.

Dingle's Bakery was welcoming and warm on a fall day, and the smell of freshly baked cookies and brewed tea of every variety drifted through the interior.

I waved at Matilda then went over to my favorite table beside the window. Jumbo sunned himself on the bench in the sun and gave me a greeting purr-meow.

"Good morning," I said, offering him a warm smile and a few tummy scratches. I retracted my hand before he got irritated or playful.

Matilda finished up with her customer and came over to join me. "I've got a new tea in stock," she said, and gave me a hug. "Rosehip. Can I interest you?"

"What magical properties does it have?" I asked.

Matilda offered me a smile. "It boosts your immune system and makes your skin look healthier. Among other things." She wriggled her eyebrows conspiratorially. "What do you say? Rosehip tea and cookies?"

"Sounds great."

"I'll be right back. We've got *a lot* to talk about," she said.

My eyes widened, but Matilda strode off before I could ask her what she'd meant. A lot to talk about? Matilda wasn't a huge gossip, but she'd always helped me with my cases. She'd also set up a camera in her apartment upstairs to view the street out front and catch any strange happenings during the night and day.

Mostly because she was concerned about Jumbo's safety.

Looking at the cat, I didn't see why. It wasn't like Jumbo had ever made a bid for escape. He was a pampered, happy cat.

I settled back in my comfy chair then rooted around in my purse for my phone. I wanted to write up a to-do list or memo about the case. I wasn't going to let Shawn bully me out of figuring this out, not after Aunt Sof had begged me for help.

"Here you go, rosehip tea with cookies," Matilda said. "They've got strawberry preserves in them."

I thanked her and took a sip of the fragrant tea. The stress on my shoulders eased. "This is soothing," I said. "Thank you."

Matilda rewarded me with a happy dance. There was nothing she enjoyed more than helping others. She joined me and took a bite of a cookie, a look of barely contained excitement on her face.

"What?" I asked. "Come on, what is it? You can't tell me that we have *a lot* to talk about and then not tell me what it is."

Matilda set her cookie down on the table, spilling crumbs left and right and not caring about it in the least. Jumbo saw his opportunity and jumped down to lick them up off the floor.

"You know I'm not the type of person who spreads

gossip around," she said, "but when I saw this, I had to show you. It's got the whole town abuzz. Every customer who's come in this morning has asked me about it."

"About what?"

"The website," Matilda said. "It's a gossip website, created by someone in town, nobody knows who, and it's called The Basil Buzzer."

I took a bite of a cookie and the sweet and tart strawberry preserves spread over my tongue, paired with the delicious crumbly goodness of the vanilla cookie. "A gossip website. OK? So? No offense, but what's the big deal?"

"This." Matilda brought her phone out of the front pocket of her apron and set it in front of me. She tapped around and then navigated toward the website in question. "Look for yourself."

The website was entirely black. Black with white writing. And I'd thought Aunt Sofia's list was eye-torture.

I rubbed my eyes and pinched my fingers on the screen, zooming in on the text.

This is not a drill. This is not what you think it is. This is not what you want to hear. But this is exactly what you will hear because you need the truth.

"What does that even mean?" I murmured.

"Weird, right?" Matilda asked, leaning over to read along with me. "It popped up last night."

"No," I said. "You're kidding. Just overnight?"

"It popped up overnight and then people started getting emails about it," Matilda continued. "I checked my inbox this morning, but I didn't get a link. I'm not sure whether to be relieved or worried. Click there." She pointed to a button near the top of the page.

I clicked it, and another web page opened.

This one had a picture at the top that took time to load.

Whoever had built this site clearly didn't know how to build websites. My business and consultation brain threatened to take over, and I had to bring myself back into line.

"Who is the picture—" I cut off as it finished loading.

Romeo Moretti scowled back up at me, one corner of his lip lifting. He held a placard bearing his name. A mugshot. Romeo Moretti's mugshot.

"What the—?"

"It gets worse," Matilda whispered. "Keep scrolling."

I scrolled down the page and read the write up underneath.

Romeo Moretti. Danger to Lake Basil and all its residents.

He has a secret that he doesn't want anyone to know. If you want to find out what it is, you're going to have to come back when I announce it.

And underneath that was a timer that counted down toward zero.

"Wow. What the heck?"

"Right?" Matilda took a bite of her cookie and chewed enthusiastically. Jumbo meowed at her, jumped into her lap, and sniffed around. She stroked him absently. "This is crazy. It's like a gossip site but worse."

"The weird thing is... Hold up." I clicked through the pages of the website. "No privacy policy. No terms of service. No product. No advertising. This isn't a site that's aimed at making money. This is just... malicious."

"What do you mean?"

"The person who made this site clearly isn't monetizing it," I said. "Unless they have plans to in the future. I'm not sure how, though." I paused, thinking hard. "To me, it kind of seems like whoever did this wants to cause damage and that's about it. Damage to Moretti's reputation." And while I wasn't a fan of Romeo or the Moretti family, I didn't understand why someone would do this.

A business enemy?

Has the sight been set up specifically to target Romeo, or would there be other content too? Content targeted at more of the townsfolk?

I studied the text again, trying to muddle through why this had happened. So soon after the death of Thea, as well. Could it be a coincidence? Why would—?

"There's been an update!" a customer cried.

Most of the patrons of Dingle's Bakery were on their phones, and judging by the flashes of black on their screen, they were all visiting the same website.

"Quick," Matilda said, "refresh."

Ten

I DID AS MATILDA HAD ASKED AND REFRESHED the website, navigating back to the home page where we'd first landed. A second link had appeared in the menu bar at the top. This one had a new label.

Matilda Dingle.

Matilda's eyes went round as donuts.

And it was then that I realized most of the noise in the bakery had stopped. People were staring at Matilda, some of them with expressions that weren't happy.

Jumbo meowed in the quiet.

I clicked on the tab with an air of ripping the Band-Aid off. If this gossiper had something negative to say about my friend, some evil secret to share that she wasn't ready to be out in the open, if they had hurt her in any way, I would hunt them down. I would find them and pepper spray them right in the eyes.

Two spots had appeared in Matilda's cheeks. She didn't say anything but an air of urgency surrounded her. Fear.

A picture of Matilda, complete with the hair streaked gray, wearing her favorite shade of pink pastel with Jumbo in her arms. It wasn't a mugshot at least. But then, I was pretty sure Matilda had never been arrested.

I scrolled down.

Matilda Dingle. I know your dirty secret. Soon, everyone else will know it too.

And beneath that line was another timer, counting down to zero. It would hit zero before the Moretti timer.

Matilda blinked, staring at the words. Jumbo purred and rubbed against her arms as if he could sense her unhappiness. He wanted her attention, or he wanted to calm her down. Either way, it wasn't working.

Whispers started up in the bakery.

"What's she hiding?" someone murmured.

"She should just tell us. We're going to find out in a couple of hours anyway," a female customer said loudly.

Several others agreed with her, glaring at the back of Matilda's head.

"There's no use hiding the truth if we're just going to find out."

"Hey," I snapped, and every eye focused on me. "You don't talk about her or to her like that. What are you crazy? Have you all lost your darn minds? This website crops up and you're all so willing to trust that whoever made it has the best interest of Lake Basilites at heart? Try employing some critical thinking." I couldn't help the anger coursing through me. This was Matilda we were talking about. She'd been nothing but good and kind to me from the start. "You should be ashamed of yourselves. Here you sit in her bakery, eating her cookies and drinking her tea, demanding secrets from her when—"

Matilda took hold of my arm and squeezed. "It's OK, Gina. I've got this."

"But—"

"The truth will set you free," she whispered, then rose and faced the bakery full of customers. "I don't have much to hide. You know I'm not from Lake Basil," she started.

A few people narrowed their eyes at me, others looked genuinely abashed after my lecture.

"I'm not from Lake Basil," she continued, "and in the name of transparency, I'll tell you my two secrets."

"Matilda," I said.

But she shook her head at me.

This wasn't right. People were allowed to have their secrets. Not everybody had to know everything all the darn time.

"This is important," Matilda said. "Important to me and to them." She took a deep breath. "My first secret is that I came to Lake Basil because I wanted to escape my ex-husband. He was a mean, horrible man who... Well, it wasn't an easy marriage, and I needed an escape. I'm lucky he even signed the divorce papers. He was arrested and put in prison a few years ago."

Everyone gasped or murmured.

This made me even angrier. This was intensely private stuff that she *didn't* have to share.

"The only reason I'm telling you this, is not because I'm worried about what it says on that website, it's because I've been living in the shadow of my past for too long. I've been afraid he'll get out of prison and find me. I've been making myself small, and I'm not going to do that anymore." She squared her shoulders.

People shifted at their tables, some smiling, some uncomfortable. Served them right for demanding the truth from her.

"Now, the second secret," she said, "is more relevant."

That got their attention.

"Only a few people know about it," Matilda said, "but I have several cameras set up watching the bakery from every angle."

Gasps.

"Not interior cameras, exterior ones. Watching the

street and my bakery," Matilda said. "So that I can keep Jumbo safe." And then she sat down in her seat, breathing heavily.

Silence moved through the bakery like a living thing.

And then...

"That's not so bad," somebody said.

"Can't say I wouldn't do the same if I had a cat and could afford it."

"Might even help keep the crime down in the street."

And then the hubbub resumed as people turned back to the website and began discussing what Moretti's secret might be.

"That was wrong," I said. "It's not fair that you have to share your secrets."

"I guess it doesn't matter whether it's fair or not," Matilda said, stroking Jumbo, who settled in her lap again after the interruption. "What matters is that I took the power away from this stranger who wants to share things about my life. Now, it doesn't matter what they put on that website, the people of this town know exactly who I am."

That was true. I clicked my fingers. "And if they publish a lie about you," I said, "we can find out who runs the website and sue them for defamation of character."

"Don't there technically have to be damages to my business or finances for that to work?"

"Darn you for always being so rational," I said.

I wanted to retaliate against whoever had made this site. I had to take a breath and take stock of everything that had happened. It didn't help to get so worked up over things I couldn't control.

The door opened, the bell tinkling above it, and a woman entered.

She wore her hair poker straight and raven, and she was so tall, I imagined she'd had to duck on her way through the door. She wore a long black dress and had paired it with a cloak. I half expected her to produce a poisoned apple and try to tempt someone with it. Except she was nothing like a crone. She was painfully beautiful, almost, with rose-red lips, and an imperious stare.

"Who on earth is that?" I whispered, more to myself than to Matilda.

A few people had glanced up, but the chatter hadn't stopped. The regulars all knew her. How come I didn't? Sure, I hadn't been back in Lake Basil for that long, but this was the type of woman who stood out in a crowd.

"Oh, that's Joanie Winters," Matilda said. "Comes in every other day to grab my tea special of the week. I'll be right back."

A shocked cry rang out before Matilda had taken two steps.

"There's been another update!"

Murmurs erupted in the interior of the bakery as everyone turned their gazes to their phone screens yet again.

Eleven

GINA ROMANO.

The tab had appeared at the top of the web page. I almost didn't want to click it, even though it would probably be a write-up about my secrets and a timer counting down to their reveal.

But my tab wasn't the only one that had appeared.

Beau Henderson.

The guesthouse owner had his own tab, and that was even more alarming and interesting than the fact that I had one myself.

The newcomer, Joanie, produced a phone from within her cape. "An update?" she squawked. "Again? Whoever's running this site has a lot of time on their hands."

I couldn't help but agree with her.

And I didn't like the sight of my name in the menu bar.

I clicked on it, and a page opened, showing an image of me in the restaurant, standing behind the hostess stand and tapping away on my tablet. It looked recent.

A cold chill ran down my spine.

What the heck? Was this the murderer stalking the town's residents? Why post about random people in town?

The text underneath my picture was accompanied by another of those timers counting down.

Gina Romano seems like a sweet, innocent and dedicated restaurant owner. But she's got a deep, dark secret that you'll soon find out about.

Again, I could sense the wary eyes of the customers on me.

I tossed my hair. "If you think I'm going to tell you anything about myself, you're out of your darn minds, you hear me?" I'd accidentally channeled a bit of Uncle Rocco's blustery energy there. He wouldn't put up with these shenanigans and neither would I.

The customers returned to their chatter and gossiping, leaving me in relative peace to open the other new tab about Beau.

This one loaded a massive picture of Beau with his arm around—

My jaw dropped.

His arm was around Thea. The victim. I'd known the pair had been friends, but I hadn't realized they'd been this close. Another timer accompanied the write-up.

Beau Henderson thinks he can keep his secret forever, but it's only a matter of time until the truth comes out...

"Well," Joanie said from the front counter of the bakery, "clearly somebody's got an ego issue. Putting up secrets about people? He's sent the town into a tailspin."

"You're assuming it's a man?" The words left my mouth before I could think too much about them.

Joanie flashed me a pretty smile, and I got up and went over, abandoning my tea and half-eaten cookie. I didn't have that much of an appetite left after these website revelations. Or lack thereof.

I shook Joanie's dainty hand and introduced myself.

"Oh, you own the restaurant across the street, right? I've been meaning to try the place," Joanie said. "But I'm afraid cheese doesn't agree with me. Lactose intolerant." She pulled a face. "Which is a pity since I'm a sucker for a good ice cream."

"We can take your dietary requirements into account," I said. "We have vegan dishes. But I wouldn't worry about hard cheese like parmesan too much. Doesn't have much lactose in it."

"Oh, trust me, I'm sensitive. I'd spend the night in the

restaurant restroom rather than enjoying the food." Joanie blushed. "Sorry. That was crass."

I laughed. "It's not a big deal," I said, then turned to Matilda. "I should probably head out soon. I want to check on Aunt Sof. She hasn't been the same since Thea..."

"I heard about that," Joanie murmured. "Heard there was a big memorial service for her. I didn't know her personally, but I heard she was a lovely lady."

"She was nice," Matilda said. "She loved the people in this town and they loved her back."

"Apart from one person, apparently," I said softly.

Joanie pressed a hand to her mouth. "Is it true that she was stabbed?"

"That's what we heard," I said carefully. I didn't know Joanie well, and I didn't want any of my information traveling through the masses of gossips behind me. I didn't blame them for being intrigued with the website—Lake Basil was small, and there wasn't much to do in the colder months—but that didn't mean I trusted them.

"That's horrible," Joanie murmured through her fingers. "Do you think—Well, I mean, surely the police have a solid lead on the case. They won't just let a murderer run around free and wild on the streets."

An image of a man wearing a hoodie and holding a

knife appeared in my mind, except he was gamboling through the streets of Lake Basil happily, waving his arms around. "I don't know about free and wild," I said, trying not to smile. "But I'm sure they've got something to keep them occupied."

As if I'd summoned him, the door to the bakery opened, and Shawn entered.

If the silence after the reveal of Matilda's secrets had been great, it was nothing compared to the quiet that spread through the bakery now.

Shawn sniffed and adjusted his jeans. "Morning," he said, nodding around at everyone. "Morning."

The townsfolk greeted back, but whispers started up the minute he reached the counter.

"Morning, ladies." He met my gaze for a split-second before he glanced away. "Joanie."

"You two know each other?" I asked.

"Oh yeah," Joanie said. "Quite well, actually." There was a flirty quality to her voice.

The tips of Shawn's ears had turned pink. That was interesting. *Then maybe it wasn't Shawn who left a rose on my doorstep?*

Rose? Try *roses*. But if not him, then it had to be whoever had murdered Thea right? Except Thea might have picked up the rose anywhere.

"What can I get for you this morning, Detective?" Matilda asked. "I was just about to grab Joanie's order of rosehip tea. Would you like—?"

"No. No, thank you," he said briskly. "I wanted to talk to you, Matilda. In private."

"Oh. Uh, OK," she said, frowning and shooting me a glance. "Is this about what happened to Thea?"

Again, Shawn went pale and started shifting around. The change from commanding to unhappy was so stark I could scarcely believe it. What was it about? Why—?"

"I'll ask Tina to take over," Matilda said, and waved over one of her servers. And then she guided Shawn back to the door that led up to her apartment. Joanie and I watched in silence together as they disappeared from sight.

"So, are you and the detective, uh, dating?" I asked Joanie.

"Us? Oh, no!" Joanie laughed like the idea was ludicrous. "I'm not interested in men. They're more trouble than they're worth. But he is a sweet man, isn't he?" She accepted her order from Tina then said goodbye and headed out the door and into the crisp fall morning.

I was tempted to wait around for Matilda, but I had no idea how long they would be. And I desperately wanted to discuss the website with my aunt.

She'd be eager to talk about it, and she might have

some information that I could use in my case. Especially now that I'd seen that picture of Beau and Thea together. Had Romeo Moretti been telling the truth?

Twelve

THE DRIVE OVER TO AUNT SOFIA'S HOUSE WAS
far less eventful than my visit to the bakery, but it was
interesting.

Mostly because when I turned the corner into my aunt
and uncle's street, I spotted a beautiful young woman
striding down the sidewalk, holding a rose and smiling to
herself. Was it just rose season? Or was there a more
sinister reason there were so many roses around?

Rosehip tea. Roses on my doorstep. A rose at the
crime scene. And now a woman with a rose in my aunt and
uncle's street.

I parked the Lexus and found my Aunt Sofia in the
front yard, tottering around with her gloves on. They were
caked in dirt. She spotted me and set her trowel aside.
"There you are, Gina, honey. I've been waiting for you to

come by. Did you see that new website? Can you believe it? What do you think?"

"I don't know what to think." I searched the street for the woman, but she was long gone.

"Your name is on that website. It seems like whoever made it is publishing a new update every hour," Aunt Sofia said.

"More frequently than that," I said. "There have been like three updates in the past hour alone. And Beau was one of them."

"Beau?" Aunt Sofia stripped off her garden gloves and set them aside.

We entered the hall and moved past the living room where Uncle Rocco was watching a nature documentary. It was better for his blood pressure than sports, and he was half-asleep when I popped in to give him a quick kiss on the cheek as a greeting.

Aunt Sofia directed me to a chair at the kitchen table then set about making us a pot of coffee. She opened a container full of cookies and put them on the table.

"Ginger cookies," she said, with an impish grin. "Rocky can't stand them so he won't eat them, no matter how desperate he gets for sugar."

"Devious." I grabbed one, took a bite and enjoyed the zing and sugary goodness.

Aunt Sofia sat down while she waited for the coffee to

brew. "I've been thinking a lot about that list I gave you," she said. "Writing it was difficult for me, and I get that Thea had a lot of enemies now. But I still can't believe she's gone."

"*A lot* of enemies," I said, pulling my phone out and opening my email to look at the list my aunt had forwarded me. "So many I'm not sure where to start."

"Romeo Moretti is where you start," she said instantly. "Especially now that his name is up on the website. Gosh, I remembered something this morning." She licked her fingers then rushed from the room.

"OK…" I shook my head and clicked through to the gossip website again, my heart pounding. The timer on my "secret" wasn't up yet, but the one on Romeo's was.

And the information printed underneath his picture made my blood run cold.

Romeo Moretti has a rap sheet longer than both your arms. He's been arrested multiple times for aggravated assault, he's a felon who is out on parole, he's dangerous, and he has a firearms license. Romeo will kill you for dispersing his secrets.

Romeo plans on starting a crime syndicate in Lake Basil. He wants to take the Moretti family's ill-gotten gains and multiply them by laundering money through the now-closed Moretti's Italian restaurant. You've been warned.

Stay away from Moretti. Pray that the corrupt police in this town will be cleaned up so that he'll be arrested.

Consider this your public service announcement. Stay tuned for more information on this.

"Holy…" I read it all again, shaking my head.

I'd know Romeo had priors after checking him out in the past, but this was a lot. To be fair, I had *suspected* that Moretti was up to something when I'd seen the business associates he moved with in town, but this?

To have it all printed out in literal black and white for the entirety of Lake Basil, no, the world, to see?

Romeo had to be fuming. He had to be—

"Here." Aunt Sofia reentered the kitchen and placed her phone in front of me. "These are some texts that Thea sent me a while ago. I had to scroll far back to find them. This was weeks before she was… Before *it* happened."

I took the phone from my aunt.

Hi Thea. Everything OK? You sounded strange on the phone.

Yeah, I don't know…

What's wrong, honey? You know you can tell me anything.

I trust you, Sof. I do. I'm just a little scared. I've got the feeling that Romeo Moretti wants to… do something to me.

What do you mean?

I don't know. He's just mean.

Romeo's mean? We all know that. :)

Yes, but he's being particularly mean. Anyway, it's probably nothing. See you at book club!

Can't wait!

And the conversation after that was more mundane. "Wow," I said. "This is bad. Especially after what I read." I pressed my phone across the table and Aunt Sof gave it a read, pulling the phone close to her face and then away in an effort to focus. She murmured about reading glasses and wandered out of the room again.

This was getting complicated.

First, Moretti was found standing over the body. Then he claimed that Beau was the murderer, and that he'd heard Thea being stabbed. But his timeline didn't make sense.

Then there was the fact that there had been a rose found on the body, and, most important of all, Moretti had been *following* Thea in the early morning hours.

Why?

Had Thea, who loved gossip and knowing things

about other people, known about Moretti's plans to establish a crime syndicate in Lake Basil?

If that was the case, could it be as simple as the fact that Moretti wanted to get rid of Thea before she could out him?

And why on earth were there roses everywhere? What was that about?

The longer this went on, the more serious things became—if Moretti was the murderer, and he might not be, then there was the chance that he would strike again, specifically, he would strike out at the creator of the website that had outed his plans.

But what if all the website information was a lie?

Aunt Sofia entered the kitchen with her glasses, shock written all over her face. "They've just published an update about poor Matilda."

"What does it say?"

"That she has cameras watching the residents of Lake Basil," Aunt Sofia replied.

"Anything else? Anything at all?"

"No," Aunt Sofia said. "But I can't believe this is happening, Gina. There's some kind of sicko among us, sharing everybody's secrets. What if they start talking about Rocky? Or me?"

"Don't worry, Auntie, I'm going to figure this out."

"This is scary," Aunt Sofia said, sitting down and grabbing a ginger cookie. She took a bite and crunched noisily, for once unworried by where she spilled crumbs.

"I know," I said. "But I'm going to put a stop to this." I had to find whoever had created this website before it was too late.

Not because I was angry about them outing everyone's secrets—that too—but because they were in grave danger.

If they accidentally or intentionally outed the murderer, they would be dead. The manner in which Thea had died—repeated stab wounds—said that this person, whoever they were, was vicious and willing to do whatever it took to keep their secrets in the dark.

Thirteen

I TAPPED MY FINGERS ON THE STEERING WHEEL OF the Lexus, a mixture of confusion and concern mingling in the pit of my stomach. I wasn't about to open that website again and check what had been said about *me*, but the countdown on Beau's tab was almost done.

A sense of pressure had settled thanks to this new website.

It felt as if time was running out. The longer it took me to figure out who had started it, and who the murderer was, the more secrets would be revealed. Secrets of innocent people. For the most part. Did Romeo Moretti *count* as an innocent person?

I tabbed away from the website on my phone and opened my trusty memo that I had saved on my home screen.

To-do List:

- *Stock issue with cheese supplier. Consider finding a new one??*
- *Narrow down suspects list.*
- *Figure out who could have been in the area on the morning of Thea's death.*
- *Roses???*
- *Romeo Moretti? Beau? Who else? People staying at the guesthouse?*

Or could it be as simple as it being Moretti? He was the one who had been found standing over the victim's body, and he had reason to hate her.

Thea had to have known his secret. It was the only reason he could've been following her. If she knew that he planned on starting a crime syndicate in Lake Basil, well, that was more than enough to kill her over.

He'd blamed Beau because he wanted a scapegoat.

But something about that didn't sit right with me. I couldn't place my finger on it, but it felt as if I'd missed a step—that stomach-swooping feeling of stepping further than intended.

Beau. What about Beau?

The picture on the website had made it clear that Beau had a pretty close relationship with Thea. It stood to reason then, that he might have known her secrets too. But what secret could Beau have been hiding that would have possibly warranted him murdering her?

It didn't fit either. Beau was a sweetheart. He'd always been kind to me, and he had a wife. No reason for him to be *too* involved in Thea's life. Or leave her a rose for instance.

And then there was Shawn. I couldn't rule him out either.

It felt absurd to even think that, but Shawn was acting stranger than usual. Talking to Matilda about the murder, weirdly enough, leaving me roses and then threatening me.

Was it possible that Shawn had done something?

I shook my head. I didn't want to believe one of the Lake Basilites who had been hired to protect our community would instead harm it, but I had to live in the real world. Corrupt cops existed. They were human too.

I navigated back to the Basil Buzzer website, my heart beating out an uneven rhythm.

The site had updated again. Beau's countdown had come to an end. There were three new tabs that had cropped up in the last half an hour, each with a timer of their own. One for Joanie, the beautiful cloak-wearing woman from the bakery, one for Shawn, and one for Lou, who had been there on the morning of the murder.

Uh oh.

I opened Beau's page, bracing myself.

This is Beau Henderson, owner of the Lake Basil Guesthouse. But you already knew that. What you didn't know, however, is that Beau was good friends with Thea, the victim of a recent senseless crime. Beau also hit Thea with his car two years ago. Beau is the reason that Thea had a limp. Thea never pressed charges against Beau because they were such good friends, but Beau hasn't driven a car since it happened.

I re-read the write-up, swallowing at the implication.

Beau had hit Thea with his car.

That didn't mean he was a bad person, just a terrible driver. Especially if Thea had chosen not to press charges against him.

The more I thought about it, the more I needed to get over to the guesthouse and chat to Beau about what had happened. I'd have to be careful—I didn't need Shawn coming down on me like a sack of bricks.

I refreshed the site one last time.

There hadn't been any updates in the past ten minutes, which was a good sign. Maybe the mystery website creator had run out of secrets to disperse?

"You're not seriously going to do this," I whispered to myself, my finger hovering over the tab that bore my name.

I was nervous.

It was silly. I didn't have anything to hide, did I?

Surely, the creator of the website wouldn't know anything bad about me? Then again, they could make up total lies and—

I clicked on the tab before I could chicken out.

Gina Romano, owner of Romano's Family Restaurant, has made it her life mission to bring down the Moretti family. She also likes to investigate active police cases even though she knows that it will endanger herself and her family. She might seem like she has a soft and sweet exterior, but her dark secret is that she's currently involved with two men. Jacob, the chef at her restaurant and long time boyfriend, and Shawn, the detective from the Lake Basil Police Department.

The shriek of anger that sprung from my lips startled a woman passing by my car.

Who on earth would write something like this? It wasn't true! I wasn't involved with Shawn. If Jacob saw this...

I forced myself to take deep breaths. If Jacob saw this, he would know it wasn't true.

But isn't it true? Why haven't you told Jacob about the roses?

That evil little voice in my head scratched at me.

I fought back against it. I hadn't told Jacob about the roses because I hadn't wanted to worry him! And because he might not have been the one sending the roses

—a fact backed up by Thea having had a rose on her corpse.

Frustration welled up inside me and tears built in the corners of my eyes. None of this was fun or fair, but I wasn't going to let it get me down.

I was a City girl, and when a City girl was faced with a problem, she fixed it before it could fix her.

I pulled my phone out of my purse and sent off a text to Jacob.

> I don't know if you saw that article on the new website, but I'm not having an affair with Shawn.

> I didn't think you were. ;)

> Good. I can't believe the rumors people will make up.

> Love you. Don't stress about it.

A wave of guilt beset me. The rumors had probably come from Shawn leaving those roses on my doorstep, or the way he acted around me.

Enough was enough. I was going to get to the bottom of this. I needed to talk to Beau and figure out if he had seen anything on the morning of Thea's death. If he had been on the guesthouse porch as Romeo had claimed, then he had to have at least witnessed *something*.

Fourteen

THE LAKE BASIL GUESTHOUSE WAS SEATED among trees, with a wraparound porch that guests loved to frequent, and a sunny attached room that was perfect during the fall and a hell sauna during the summer.

I parked my car in the same spot as last time, conscious of the fact that the screens and tape were gone from the lake shore. The grassy embankment was littered with the first leaves of fall in hues of orange and yellow and red. Those splashes of crimson made me uncomfortable, but I shook it off and turned my attention to the guesthouse.

There were no cars parked out front. Either the guesthouse was struggling during fall, or everyone who was staying there had decided to dip out for breakfast or to explore what Lake Basil had to offer—cute boutique stores, the local museum, and the lake itself.

I got out of the Lexus as a gust of wind swept by me, tugging at my scarf and fluttering the end of it free from my neck. The creak of the tire swing shifting underneath the old oak gave me a chill.

I locked the car and started toward the guesthouse.

A croaking-caw stopped me in my tracks, and I spun around, searching for the source of the noise.

I found it in the oak tree, near the very top, sitting and watching me. The crow. There weren't that many crows in Lake Basil, but this had to be a coincidence, right? It couldn't be the same crow from our breakfast the other morning, could it?

The crow cawed a second time, and then — "Out. Get out!" Its throat warbled, the black sleek feathers lifting and settling. "Out of here."

So, it knew more words than the ones it had used the last time we'd encountered it. "No," I said, "I won't. And you can't stop me from leaving either." Great, now I was having a confrontation with a crow. "You know what? You can get out of here."

"Out!"

I took a step toward it, but a slam from inside the guesthouse made me stumble. The crow took flight, disappearing off over the lake in the direction of my house.

"Yeah," I said, "that's what I thought. Don't start

something and it won't be something!" I shouted that part after the crow like an absolute loon, then strode toward the guesthouse. What an unsettling day.

First the website, then Shawn interviewing Matilda, and now a crow taunting me.

I mounted the porch steps, shaking my head at the ridiculousness of this situation and entered the reception area.

I stopped dead in my tracks.

A scream left my lips before I could stop it.

Beau lay on the floor in a pool of blood, face down. Too much blood for him to be alive.

BEAU'S BODY HAD BEEN REMOVED FROM THE guesthouse on a covered stretcher. He was dead, and even though I'd called 911 immediately, followed their directions, and tried to help, there was nothing anyone could do.

I sat on a porch swing, still as a statue, staring at the lake, my mind racing. Every time I blinked, I'd see an image of Beau's body.

This was horrifying.

Not only was Beau, another of the pillars of our Lake

Basil community, gone, but he'd been stabbed just like Thea. That had to mean it was the same killer.

So Beau obviously hadn't been the one to do it, which made sense since he wouldn't have had a reason if he was friends with her and she had never pressed charges for him striking her with his car or demanded money from him or the like.

But why would she have wanted to press charges against him unless he had done it intentionally?

I pressed my hand over my mouth and held it there. The contact between my palm and face warmed me and gave me comfort. Everything around me was a blur, and I sat back, trying not to panic.

Beau dead. Thea dead. Roses. A crow. Shawn. Moretti.

The mantra repeated in my head several times.

Why kill Beau? Why kill Thea?

The two deaths had to be connected.

There hadn't been a rose on Beau's body, but they had both been stabbed viciously. Someone had wanted them out of the way and had been willing to kill to achieve their end goal. But who and why?

I wasn't sure that stabbing matched Romeo's personality. He was a smooth operator, but he had a temper. If not him, then who else? I would have to go over my aunt's list and take another look at that website.

Could it be that the murderer had started it to

throw people off their scent? But surely the cops could figure out who had created the website. Things like that left a footprint. Websites had to have hosting, a login with an email address attached, a registered domain name and—

"Gina." Shawn's voice cut through my thoughts.

I dropped my hand from my mouth. "Shawn." He was the last person I wanted to talk to right now, especially after the way he'd acted at the restaurant.

Shawn sighed, touching a hand to his ID badge before settling his palms against the railing behind him. He leaned on it, studying me.

I didn't say anything and stared right back. If he accused me of something, I would lose it. The man couldn't be serious.

"Gina, I need to talk to you about what happened here today and take your statement."

I nodded.

"I need to know exactly what happened and in which order," Shawn said roughly. "Got it?"

"Yeah."

"Good. Let's get started."

Tension took hold of my shoulders, but I ignored his mean attitude and told him exactly what had happened from the moment I'd arrived at the guesthouse to when I'd found the body and called 911.

Shawn listened with impatience that I didn't appreciate.

Afterward, he tilted his head to one side, sweeping his gaze over me like he could will me to give more detail. "That's it?"

"Yeah."

Shawn cleared his throat. "I'm struggling here, Gina."

"With what?"

"With understanding why you think a crow in a tree has any bearing on what happened to Beau," Shawn said.

I bristled. "You told me to tell you everything that happened. That includes the darn crow in the darn oak tree."

"For future reference, I would prefer it if you left out animals when you're telling me—"

"Am I free to go?" I didn't care about being rude. Beau was dead, and the detective was more interested in mocking me over how I gave a statement than taking the case seriously.

"Yeah, but—"

"Good." I got up slowly, in case I got a case of the faints, but I was sturdy. I walked down the front steps of the guesthouse and headed toward my car. I couldn't handle much more of this. The town had lost two of its greatest community members, and all Shawn could do was go pale and sweaty or fixate on the things I said.

It was like he had a personal vendetta against me.

No rose. Why no rose?

The words moved through my mind, loosely attached to each other and making barely any sense, but I was sure they were important.

Fifteen

That night, late...

JACOB AND I ARRIVED HOME AFTER A LONG DAY at the restaurant, and I could barely keep my eyes open. It was a pity then, that whenever they closed, I'd catch a glimpse of Beau's body. There had been murders in Lake Basil before, bodies and crime scenes that I had witnessed, terrible things that I wanted to forget. This time around, I hadn't seen Thea's body, and I'd been relieved. But now Beau...

Jacob parked the car in front of our lake house and took hold of my hand. He squeezed. "Are you OK?"

"I—I think so," I said. "I'm frazzled. Been through the ringer today, you know?"

Jacob nodded. "You look exhausted."

"Yeah." It was just the truth. "But I don't know if I'll be able to sleep. Every time I shut my eyes…"

Jacob pressed a hand to my cheek. "All right, so let's stay up a while. I'll make you some hot chocolate and a snack, and we can talk about what happened. Maybe that will help you process it?"

It should've been the last thing that I wanted to do, but the thought of talking about it helped. Maybe we would figure something out together.

Jacob circled to the passenger door and opened it for me, offering me a hand. He helped me out, and we walked to the front door together. And stopped.

And stared.

At the rose on the doorstep with a card attached.

"What's this?" Jacob asked.

I sighed as he picked it up.

He read the card. "Sorry for the way I acted today." Jacob frowned. "Gina?"

"That," I said, "is the reason that everyone thinks I'm having an affair with Shawn. That's my best guess, anyway. He's been leaving me roses on the doorstep for a month now, even though I told him I'm not interested and I'm committed to you."

Anger flashed across Jacob's features. "He… what?"

"I didn't tell you," I said, "because I didn't want you to get angry or stressed about it, and I figured he'd stop, eventually. I mean, surely the man will save what's left of his darn dignity and leave me alone."

Jacob shook his head.

I took the rose from him, removed the card and tossed the flower aside. I tore up the card. "I'm sorry for not telling you sooner," I said, "that was wrong of me, but I did have a second reason."

"A second reason?"

"Let's talk inside." I unlocked the door and went through to the kitchen to dispose of the card. Jacob joined me a second later and sat down at the kitchen table. I did the same.

"What's the second reason?" Jacob asked.

"Thea was holding a rose when she was attacked," I said. "And I was worried that Shawn was involved in the murder. That or it wasn't Shawn at all who was sending me the roses."

"But Gina, that's even more reason to tell me what's going on," Jacob said. "I'm here to protect you. I'm your fi —your boyfriend, for heaven's sake."

I ignored the Freudian slip. "I know," I said. "And I hear you. In the future, I'll talk to you about these things, but I was unsure of myself, especially since Shawn has been acting strange lately."

I told him about what had happened outside the restaurant and that I was *still* concerned that he was up to something.

Jacob reached across the table and held my hand. "Huh."

"What?"

"I don't know," Jacob said. "Shawn's a friggin'... He's an idiot, but he's usually a good cop. Even if I don't like the guy, I can see that."

"So, you think he hasn't got anything to do with it." I wanted to fight him on that. Shawn had gotten under my skin with his questions at the guesthouse today, and the way he'd been behaving over the past few months.

"I'm not saying that," Jacob said. "I think there's more to this than meets the eye."

"Yeah," I said. "But I wish I knew what the 'more to this' was, if you know what I mean." But this was just a part of the investigation, right? This happened often.

Every time I'd sleuthed out a murderer, there had been a moment during my journey toward the truth where I was either sure I was on the wrong path, or I couldn't figure things out because I was missing some crucial piece of evidence. And I felt like that now.

"Thanks for being so understanding," I said. "I know I should have told you sooner."

"I get why you wouldn't," Jacob said. "The last time

Shawn and I had words, it almost got ugly. I don't want you to think I'm some irrational dude with a bad temper. That's not me. I can't stand it when people overstep boundaries, and I feel like Shawn does that often."

"I get it."

Jacob got up from the table and circled around to my side. He kissed me on the forehead. "How about that hot chocolate?"

"With cookies?"

"You bet."

"You're the best, Jake." I grabbed his hand and squeezed it. "Can I help you with anything?"

"No. You sit. You've had a rough day."

"Thank you." I busied myself with my purse on the table, pulling my phone from within because I hadn't had a chance to check on the website yet this evening. It had been a busy day after Beau's death. The news had broken. People had already started mourning and turning up to the restaurant to talk and be with each other.

The Lake Basilites were scared and unhappy, and that made me angry. This was our home, and I wouldn't let the peace stay broken.

I opened the website and frowned.

There were no new tabs at the top.

A couple of the timers had counted down to reveal the secrets they'd been hiding, but the website owner hadn't put up any new information. It was almost as if they'd just given up. Or as if they—

My eyes widened.

Was it a coincidence that Beau had died and the website posts had stopped?

But there was a post about Beau on the website. *A positive one.* And would Beau really do that to people? Put their secrets out in the world? Why?

I tapped through the tabs as I processed the new information.

The tab about Joanie Winters drew my attention.

Joanie Winters loves to keep secrets, and that's why she keeps to herself. That cloak doesn't keep the truth away, Joanie, and you should know that by now. The citizens of Lake Basil deserve to know the truth. Joanie Winters is an ex-con. She was involved with the Galliana crime family in New York before she moved to Lake Basil. She's hiding out in Lake Basil to avoid arrest. The police are going to find her though, and that's a problem for Joanie. There's evidence that she left behind that no one knows about.

There's more that you don't know about her, so stay tuned...

There was no timer underneath the post.

Shawn's tab still had a timer counting down to whatever secret he was hiding.

Was it possible that Beau was the one who had made

these posts? That he had died and there would be no further updates? I had to figure this out. I couldn't ask Beau about what he'd seen on the morning of the murder.

But I could talk to Moretti again.

Sixteen

The following morning...

JACOB SAT IN THE PASSENGER SEAT BESIDE ME, holding his phone and tapping away. I had parked across from the Moretti mansion, and my gaze was glued to the gates and the cars parked out front. Lucia's sports car was gone—I wasn't sure if the Moretti's had sold it after her passing or if it caused them too much pain to use it. Either way, it made me sad that it was gone.

Lucia had been my "enemy" in business, but she hadn't deserved to die. Especially not in the way she had passed.

I shook off the negative train of thought and turned my attention to the phone in my lap. I had Aunt Sofia's exhaustive suspect list open on it.

"Joanie," I murmured, "is on the list. Romeo is on the list. Shawn is on the list." I scratched the end of my nose. "If only I could prove any of the others were at the crime scene other than Romeo."

"He does seem like the most likely suspect," Jacob said. "Almost done, by the way."

"Thank you. You're amazing."

"All that flattery will get you more hot chocolate this evening and another cookie," he said.

I grinned. "In that case, you are the most perfect person to walk the face of the earth."

"Two cookies for you."

I laughed and turned my gaze back toward the house. The Moretti Mansion was a triple story with more rooms than I cared to think about. I'd only been inside it two or so times and one of those times had been entirely illegal. The memory of being chased out was fresh in my mind.

"If Shawn catches us here..."

"If Shawn knows what's good for him, he'll stay away from you and me," Jacob said. "Or I'll find a creative way to dispose of those roses he's been leaving on our doorstep."

I pressed my lips together to keep from laughing. "That was very euphemistic of you."

"I'm trying not to let my vindictive side show," Jacob

replied. "Got it. Yeah, the domain name is literally registered to Beau."

"You're kidding!"

"Beau's the one who set up the Basil Buzzer website," Jacob said. "Beau's the one who has been outing everyone."

"That explains why all the posts stopped," I said. "And that's probably why the murderer struck again." I gasped, clicking my fingers. "Of course. Think about it, Jake."

"Oh, I am."

"Thea was murdered because of her lack of secret-keeping skills."

"Or her expertise in secret-finding," Jacob put in.

"Exactly. And Beau was friends with her. Good enough friends that he posted about it on the site," I said. "He must have gotten all that information from her and decided to out it. Maybe because he wanted the murderer to take the fall."

"Does that mean that one of the people he outed is the murderer?" Jake asked.

"Maybe. I don't know. But it could be that he hadn't posted about the murderer yet," I said. "Or it's Joanie. He was going to give an extra update about her."

"But he did that with Moretti too," Jacob said, navigating to Moretti's page. "See? He said 'stay tuned' or whatever."

"You're right. Darn. So it could be either of them."

"Or someone else entirely."

I scrubbed my fingers through my hair, irritably. "I feel like I'm grasping for clues that aren't there. This is so frustrating."

"Look at it this way," Jacob said, "you know more now than you ever have before."

"True. But it would be great if I could have just a smidgeon more of information."

"Just a smidgeon?" Jacob held up his thumb and forefinger. "That's all. Don't be too greedy now."

"I'd settle for a crumb at this point."

Beau made the website to out information that Thea had given them, but they both died for it. Romeo Moretti had followed Thea. Could he have been at the guesthouse yesterday and I hadn't realized it? After all, there had been a banging noise inside.

Was that noise the slam of a door as Moretti made his hasty escape?

Or Shawn? Or Joanie? Or any of the other suspects on the list or on the website? The only thing I could be sure of was that this hadn't been Matilda.

"Movement," Jacob said, pointing past me to the house.

I rolled down the window a little and peeked out.

Men had emerged from the Moretti mansion and

stood on the fabulous porch between the columns, talking to each other. They wore suits, and they looked mean. The one standing beside Romeo had a scar that ran down the side of his face, puckering the skin along his cheek.

The men shook hands all around, the tone of the conversation shifting. A burst of laughter was followed by pats on the back.

More proof that Moretti was up to something—but it was the same as what we already knew. Moretti was up to no good. Big deal. He might want to use the closed restaurant as a front to launder money. Big deal—we knew that.

How did it connect to the murders? To Thea. To the rose?

"Maybe it's *him*," Jacob said, sounding as frustrated as I was.

I wanted to hug him at that moment. It was nice to have someone else stressing about the case rather than me alone.

"Maybe," I said.

The men separated and got into their cars. I was about to start mine and drive off before Moretti or any of these guys caught sight of us when the fluttering of wings came from overhead. A black feather drifted down and landed on my windshield.

"The crow," I said. "That darn crow."

"Huh?"

"The crow that pooped on my eggs, remember?"

"Yeah?" Jacob stared at me like I'd lost it.

"I've been seeing it everywhere. First at our house, then at the guesthouse, and now here."

"Are you sure it's the same crow?" Jacob asked.

I started the car and took off down the street before Moretti and his cronies came out of the gates of the mansion. "How many talking crows do you know?"

"I don't make a habit of befriending talking crows, so not many," Jacob said.

"You think I'm reading too much into crow behavior, I take it."

"You said it," he replied.

"I know, I know." And what were the chances that this crow showed up everywhere? Why had it been in the tree over my house? Why at the guesthouse? And now at the Moretti's place?

Maybe you're finally losing it. It could be someone's pet. Or it could just be a random crow that lived around the lake. After all, it wasn't like I'd seen it following me in town.

"Don't worry, Gina," Jacob said. "Whatever happens, we'll figure it out."

"I don't know what I'd do without you."

He shrugged. "Eat less cookies. Not have a chef. Chase down random crows, probably?"

I laughed. "All of those things."

Now, if only I could put the final pieces of the puzzle together and figure out why Shawn was acting weird, if Joanie had been involved in Thea's death, and whether Romeo was the killer or not.

All in a day's work, right?

Seventeen

Late that night...

I WAS DETERMINED TO STAY UP UNTIL THE TIMER hit zero.

The only page left on the Basil Buzzer that had yet to be revealed was Shawn's, and the reveal was due to take place at two in the morning. Jacob had given up waiting and decided to go to bed since he was tired after a long night at the restaurant.

I couldn't sleep.

And I went over my new notes as I considered everything that had happened over the last day or two.

Updated to-do list:

- *Prove Romeo did it (if he did do it). How? Find evidence? Knife in his house?*
- *Find out more about Joanie?*
- *Find out what Shawn is hiding and his whereabouts on the morning of Thea's death. And of Beau's stabbing.*

While Beau's murder was horrifying, it also gave me information. I could cross-reference where everybody had been on the morning of Thea's murder and during the time Beau had been stabbed. If Romeo, for instance, had been in a public place, then he couldn't be the murderer. And the same was true for my other suspects.

As for proving that Romeo had or hadn't done it—breaking into his house wouldn't be easy.

It was also illegal, but I wasn't beyond getting my hands dirty, especially since Shawn was threatening me and would continue to do so regardless of how I handled the case.

Short of stopping my investigation entirely.

A noise came from outside the sliding glass door that led out into the back yard, and I froze, listening hard.

Pecking?

I got up and moved through the kitchen, my heart leaping into my chest. *The crow.* It had to be the crow. But surely, the crow wouldn't be here.

I reached the sliding glass door and clicked on the porch lights, flooding the porch and yard in light.

Nothing. No crow. No person. Nothing.

In the distance, the moon's reflection glimmered on the placid surface of the lake.

"You *are* losing it."

I shook off the silliness and went back to the kitchen to check out the article about Shawn.

It was just about time for the counter to tick down to zero.

I took a breath and hit the button to refresh the site on my phone.

And there it was. The write-up.

Guess what you don't know about Shawn Carter? He's your beloved detective, the protector of the people of Lake Basil, but he's got secrets too. Shawn Carter is a serial dater.

"Huh?" I blinked.

A serial dater who likes to take women out on dates to different places in the county. He romances them by leaving roses on their doorsteps, and when it doesn't work, he moves on to his next target. The worst thing of all? Shawn Carter has a wife.

My jaw dropped. A strangled noise escaped my throat.

Shawn's wife lives in Bronson. She gets to see her husband when he comes home on weekends and believes that he's a good man who only wants to provide for their family.

She has no idea that he's actually cheating on her with multiple women and is pursuing them relentlessly.

And that was it.

No message of more to come.

Shawn was— This couldn't be real life.

Shawn was married? But he had made such a big deal out of being in love with me. And the roses he'd left on my doorstep...

My eyes widened at the memory of the woman with the rose in town. And Thea.

I felt a little sick. I had never been interested in Shawn in that way, but to find out that a person you knew had such a dark secret was sickening. His poor wife.

Hold up, wait a second. Remember your write-up on the site?

Mine had been a lie. I wasn't in a love triangle with Shawn and Jacob, and I certainly wasn't having an affair. Did that mean that the information about Shawn, or any of the others, might be a lie too?

Or was it close to the truth? An assumption?

There hadn't been any updates on the website since Beau's death. All the counters had ticked to zero. All the information was out.

Whoever had killed Beau had wanted his updates to stop.

Was there a world in which Shawn, the detective, had decided to take matters into his own hands?

People had killed for less.

&

"Can you believe it?" Vi asked me before noon the next day.

I'd had a fitful night of sleep, irritated by my lack of leads in the case. If only I could *find* the murder weapon.

Three main suspects? If I cross-referenced the list of names on the Basil Buzzer, with the list of suspects Aunt Sofia had given me, I had three people who might have had reason to cause Thea harm. Especially if I considered the fact that Beau had gotten every scrap of information he had published from Thea.

Beau wasn't a gossip. He hadn't had his ear to the ground. But he had been best friends with—

"Gina?"

I cleared my throat. "Sorry, Vi. What were you saying?"

"Can you believe what that website said about Shawn?" Vi asked. "I mean, I know all that stuff isn't necessarily true, given what they said about you and stuff. But like, if he's cheating on his wife... That's wild."

"Wild," I agreed.

"I heard that he was going to get fired for it."

"You did?" I asked, my attention fully on her. "Where?"

"Oh, around town. My mom's friend works at the local newspaper and they're running an article on the new website and how scary it is that people can just give out information about other people like that. I'm just glad I don't got any beef with nobody because I did *not* want my name on the site. No offense."

"None taken," I said. "You're sure Shawn's going to be fired?" I didn't want that for him, even if he had lied to me. Even if he hadn't exactly been the best guy of late. But what if *he* was the killer? "You're sure?"

"Just what I heard," Vi said, shrugging. She meandered off to go clean the menus before we opened for lunch.

Think, Gina, think.

Beau made the website. Thea told Beau everything.

The people with the most reason to want to hide what they were up to were Romeo and Joanie who allegedly had criminal records or pasts, and Shawn with his roses. Especially since there was a rose at the crime scene. The first time around.

So, I needed to find evidence on the three of them. I needed to tie them to the crime scene. That was what they did in the movies. Tied the suspects to crime scenes, made sure they had motives.

But how did I—?

A woman appeared opposite the street, exiting Dingle's Bakery with a package in hand. She wore a long cloak and smiled to herself as she started down the street, heading toward her parked Hyundai.

"Vi," I called, my pulse fluttering. "Cover for me. I'll be right back."

Eighteen

I TAILED MY MARK IN THE LEXUS, HOPING THAT Joanie didn't know what I drove or that she wouldn't think anything of my silver car following hers for blocks. I hung back as she drove through town, stopping at Cara's Coffee to grab a cup of coffee to go, then heading to the bookstore right after.

What are you doing, Romano?

But I had to follow her. I had to know if she was involved.

And since I had no idea where Joanie lived and what she did for a living, this was my best option. If I could find evidence that she was at the crime scene or talk to her about it, I might be able to clear her or prove that she'd done it.

"Calm down, would you?" I muttered to myself, my hands slick on the steering wheel.

Joanie's car turned onto the dirt road that led around the lake. It drove past Beau's guesthouse, the road that arced upward toward the Moretti's place, all the way around to the other side of the lake near Jacob's home.

The Hyundai ahead of me slowed even more as it passed my place, and then it sped up, kicking up dirt and stones as it rattled off.

I followed it and spotted the car turning off down another dirt road that led to a property further back from the lake.

"What the—?"

I parked my car and got out, half-confused, half-convinced that Joanie was going to leap out of the bushes and attack me.

I walked the few steps toward the side-street and peered down it.

A house sat at its crest, double-story, well-looked after, with white awnings and a neat front yard. It was a pretty home, and Joanie emerged from her Hyundai outside of it. She mounted the steps, unlocked the front door and disappeared inside.

So, Joanie lived down the street? She lived right in the area where Thea had been murdered. And she had that criminal history to consider. Unless that was a lie. Judging by the house and its location, Joanie had plenty of money. That didn't mean that she wasn't a criminal. In fact, it could mean that she'd paid off the house with ill-gotten gains.

But I was getting ahead of myself.

I'd have to come back here during the evening. Or at least when she wasn't home so that I could break in and—

The front door clapped open and Joanie emerged onto the porch. She lifted a hand to her brow and stared down the road. "Hey!" Joanie yelled. "You going to come up to the house or you going to stand there all day?"

So much for thinking I'm a master at discretion.

I took a few steps up the road.

Joanie beckoned, and I walked up to meet her, squaring my shoulders.

"How are you, Gina?" she asked.

"I'm good. I—uh, I wanted to check in with you. See how you were doing," I said.

"Sure, you did." Joanie pursed crimson lips. "You totally weren't following me because you read up about me being some kind of criminal on that bogus website, right?"

"Uh."

"Yeah," Joanie said. "That's what I thought."

"Joanie—"

"Look, I'm not offended or anything," she said. "This

is why I prefer to keep to myself in this town. People think they know you after hearing a couple of rumors about you. Think it gives them a right to talk about you or—" She cut off and sighed. "I'm being rude. Do you want to come inside?" She glanced past me at the trees.

I turned to look, but she caught my arm, her grip firm but not uncomfortable. "Come on in and have some lemonade."

"Lemonade in fall?"

"I'd offer you a pumpkin spice latte," she said, "but I don't have one of those fancy barista machines."

I laughed. "I'm good, thanks. And I wasn't following you because of the rumors or the website. I saw you leaving Dingle's Bakery, and you looked upset." I was thinking on my feet here, hoping she'd buy it. "I wanted to make sure you were OK."

Joanie was quiet for a second. "You wanted to make sure I was OK."

"Yeah." Why had she repeated it like that?

"Why wouldn't I be OK?" she asked.

"Given that a woman was killed at the guesthouse recently, and then Beau right after, it stands to reason that we have to look out for each other," I said, and it sounded lame even to me. But it was the best excuse I had for tailing her.

In the past, I'd suffered because I'd been too open in

my questioning. Too obvious about wanting to investigate, and not because the cops had found out about what I'd been doing. No, it was because the murderer had been onto me.

"I'm good," Joanie said after a beat. "But I think you should mind your own business, Gina. You said how there's a murderer around and you're following people's cars around the lake. No offense, but it looks kind of suspicious."

She wasn't wrong, and I didn't *really* have a right to be offended after stalking her. "True. Well, if you're OK, I'll be on my way." I gave an awkward laugh.

"You sure you don't want to come in for something to drink?" Joanie asked, removing her cloak. She wore a pretty silk blouse underneath and a pair of black slacks. "I'll admit that I haven't made enough friends in this town and I wouldn't mind another one. Besides, if everyone around here thinks I'm some kind of *criminal* then I'm going to have to start putting those rumors to bed. I moved out to Lake Basil because I wanted to make new friends and live that perfect small town life. So, what do you say?"

"Raincheck?" I smiled. "I appreciate the offer, but I should get into town. I'm late for work at the restaurant."

"Oh right." Joanie clicked her fingers. "Romano's. I'll stop by some time. I'm in the mood for pasta."

I said goodbye to her and headed back down the road. I reached the end of it and glanced back. Joanie's front door was closed, the curtains in her windows open, but I couldn't see her inside.

The house was pretty, but I got the feeling that Joanie was up to something. Maybe it was the website. Or maybe it was a gut feeling.

Whatever she was hiding, I wanted to be the one to find out what it was. I got back into my car and drove off, winding past my house, and quietly alarmed by the fact that I hadn't even realized that Joanie had moved in down the street. Granted, I'd been living with Uncle Rocco and Aunt Sof until recently.

I checked in at home and found the doorstep free of roses or notes. Another clue. What was I missing? It felt as if there was a clue within plain sight, and if I looked for it hard enough, I would surely find it.

By the time I arrived back at the restaurant, I had made up my mind.

Tonight was the night.

I would have to make a few calls to pull it off, but it was *time.*

Nineteen

That night...

I LEFT THE LEXUS AT THE LAKE HOUSE, OPTING not to take the dirt road, but enter the woods that surrounded our house. The darkness beneath the trees was eerie, the quiet punctuated by the rustling of small critters in the underbrush and the occasional crunch of my boots on fallen leaves.

Not much longer now.

I drew my phone out of my pocket, lingering beneath an oak tree, and checked my messages with Matilda.

Ready?

All's going according to plan. I've got your back, Gina. Although, I have to admit this is one of the strangest requests I've ever gotten.

Can't thank you enough.

You don't have to thank me. I'll let you know how the night goes. Can't wait to eat the farfalle special.

Order extra mushrooms for me.

I'll get you a takeout order.

I navigated to my text chain with Jacob next.

Love you. Be careful tonight.

Don't worry, honey. I've got this. Just don't do anything I wouldn't, all right?

Does breaking and entering count?

Getting arrested does. Love you. Got to get cooking.

Love you too.

I exhaled slowly then started off again. I reached the back of Joanie's house. The porch lights were on. A car pulled up out front, and my best friend, Matilda, got out and approached the front door. She knocked once.

This was crazy.

It's crazy, but it has to work!

The door opened, and Joanie appeared wearing her cloak and a pretty dress. "Thanks for inviting me out, Matilda," Joanie said. "I thought I was going to be a pariah in this town after that article."

"Oh, that? Don't worry about that. People will get over it. Give it a week and they'll have forgotten all about that website."

Joanie laughed. "I hope so. I don't want people thinking I'm some kind of psycho criminal."

"Of course not." Matilda giggled.

Two figures walked to Matilda's car and got inside. They drove off, and I let out a breath, the retreating lights breaking the tension that had banded around my chest.

Matilda had completed her part of the plan.

The rest was up to me.

I needed to establish whether Joanie could have been at the crime scene and look for any viable connection to Thea. I had never seen them together, but clearly Thea had known something about Joanie, or else Beau would never have gotten that information about her.

My list was Joanie, Romeo Moretti, and Shawn.

Let's go.

I waited for a few minutes, breathing in the silence,

and then I set off across the grassy space that separated the treeline from the back of Joanie's house.

The lights were off inside, and I peered through a back window, cupping my hands to my face in the dark. I'd chosen black clothing for my "top secret" mission, but I doubted there would be anyone out here now that she'd left home.

I tried the back door, but it was locked. The planter next to the door was empty except for soil, and there wasn't a key underneath it.

I circled the house, checking all the windows. Locked tight.

The light on the front porch was a deterrent, but I was desperate.

I hurried up to the door and checked under the welcome mat. No spare key.

Darn it. Seemed like Joanie was the only woman in Lake Basil who took her security seriously.

I stepped back, fisting my hips and at a loss.

What now? How was I going to find anything if I couldn't get inside the house?

Trash. I could try her trash.

I walked down the steps and stopped on the front path, my hands on my hips. Was I really going to rifle through—?

A vicious croak came from above.

A black *thing* swept down and pain sprouted on my forehead. Bird wings flapped, and a vicious beak pecked at my head.

My scream was so loud, it had to have traveled across the lake.

I ran for it, waving my arms to fight off my crow enemy. The thing was following me! It had to be.

"Get off! Get off! Help!" I sprinted for the treeline.

The crow's beak hit me again and again, and I screamed and bolted between the trees, deeper into the darkness of the woods.

THUNK. I hit a tree and fell over backward, pain pounding through my body.

I lifted my hands to cover my face, fully expecting the attack to continue.

Silence.

No caws. No beak pecking.

No pain, apart from the wounds I'd already gotten from the darn bird.

I dropped my arms and stared up at the stars between the tree foliage, breathing hard. Was it *gone?* I hadn't imagined the attack.

My arms and head *hurt.* I got up, making for the house. I wasn't getting into Joanie's house tonight, and I had no idea what to do next.

AT QUARTER PAST NINE, MY PHONE RANG LOUDLY on the kitchen counter.

I jumped, flashing back to the crow attack, even though I hadn't actually sustained any injuries. Running into the tree had done more damage than the bird had, but in the dark, it had felt as if I was being eaten alive.

I grabbed my phone and answered. "Hello?"

"Gina!" Matilda's happy voice brought comfort that a mug of hot chocolate hadn't.

"Matilda. You have no idea how happy I am to hear your voice."

"Why? What's wrong? Are you OK?"

I told her about my failed mission.

Matilda made the appropriate noises, but I could tell she was holding back.

"All right," I said, "laugh already. I can tell you want to."

Matilda giggled. "You've got to admit, that's a kind of funny image. You running away from the crow, dressed in black, waving your arms around and then, wham, you run into a tree? It's like something out of a movie."

"Not any movie I'd watch," I grumbled.

"I have news for you," Matilda said. "I'm hoping it will make your failed mission worthwhile."

"I'm interested," I said.

"Joanie let it slip that she's Thea sister tonight."

My jaw dropped.

"Gina? Are you there?"

"Yeah, sorry. I'm shocked."

"I was too," she said. "We were talking at dinner about what's been happening in town recently, and she just straight told me that Thea was her sister, and that she'd moved to Lake Basil to be around her. But they were kind of estranged. She hadn't worked up the guts to tell Thea that she was in town when she died."

"Huh." That didn't make sense. "That's amazing information, Matilda, you're a star."

"Thanks," Matilda said. "But I can't take credit for it. She just kind of told me. Out of the blue."

"Interesting."

"And suspicious," Matilda said.

"My thoughts exactly. Why would she just tell you that? It's a lie, it has to be."

"How do you figure that?" Matilda asked.

"Because Thea's the one who was feeding information to Beau. Beau's the one who put up that tell-all website after Thea died," I said. "And if Thea knew *so much* about Joanie..."

"Then she had to have known her intimately," Matilda finished.

"Exactly. Unless it was all made up. That stuff about me was made up," I sighed.

This was confusing. And annoying. "I think," I said, taking a sip of my hot chocolate. "My best course of action is to figure out whether Shawn's rumor was the truth and where he was on the morning of Thea's passing and of Beau's death. Same with Romeo. If I can narrow down my list, I'll at least have *something.*"

For now, it was starting to feel like I was investigating in circles.

"You've got this, Gina," Matilda said. "I believe in you."

I appreciated the sentiment. I just wished I could bring the truth to light faster, before it was too late and another innocent Lake Basilite died.

Twenty

If Joanie was Thea's long-lost sister, that definitely placed suspicion on her shoulders. Especially if what the Basil Buzzer had claimed was true. Could it be that Thea had known Joanie's secrets and shared them with Beau, and Joanie for fear of the repercussions from the cops, had decided to get rid of her.

And Beau too.

I sat at the kitchen table the morning after the vicious crow attack, thoroughly exhausted and equally determined.

The case could be solved. Matilda was right. I couldn't afford to give up, and I wasn't going to let a deranged crow and particularly twisted mystery stop me.

I took a sip of the delicious coffee Jacob had made me and smacked my lips. "There has to be a solution that's in plain sight. I think if I cross-reference alibis for the time of Thea's murder and the time of Beau's I might be able to clear a few of my suspects."

"Good idea," Jacob said, and flipped a slice of bacon in his pan. The salty delicious smells drifted through the kitchen, and my stomach growled. Mystery-solving was hard work. "I don't know what's going to happen now that Shawn's been taken off the case."

"Wait, what?"

"Yeah," Jacob said. "Figures it would happen eventually, especially after the way he acted toward you. Threatening you when he has no right." Jacob's jaw tightened. "Guy's landed himself in trouble, no matter what the rumors say."

I wanted to feel bad for Shawn, but he was a suspect. "Right," I said. "Right, well, that's—"

The doorbell rang, and I pushed myself up from my seat. "I'll get it."

"Don't accept any flowers," Jacob called out after me.

"Knowing my luck, that crow's learned how to ring doorbells and is about to launch another attack," I said.

Jacob's laughter followed me down the hall.

I opened the door, and my face dropped.

This was worse than a crow attack. "Shawn," I said. "What are you doing here?"

Shawn wore a regular t-shirt and a pair of jeans, rather

than his usual work-smart outfit with a lanyard. He shifted a baseball cap on his head and gave me a sheepish smile. "Gina," he said. "I thought I should come by to apologize," he said. "After everything that happened, I–"

I waved a hand. "I don't know how I feel about that, Shawn," I said. "I—It's not my business, but if anything that I'm hearing is true, then I don't know if I want to talk to you about this."

"What do you mean?" Shawn wet his lips. "You mean that website? It's bogus. I didn't do anything they said I did. I don't have a wife, and I haven't been giving anyone roses."

"Wait, what? Anyone?"

"Yeah."

I didn't want to be arrogant here, but... "You mean anyone except for me?"

"What?"

"Roses," I said, "you haven't been giving anyone roses except for me."

He hesitated.

"Shawn," I said. "Just fess up already. It doesn't help that you keep lying. You threatened me about Thea. Why did you do that? Why did you—?"

"Fine," he grunted. "Maybe I have been handing out roses to women, but I'm not married. I'm a single man. I can do what I want, and I—"

"You made me feel really uncomfortable," I said. "You know that I'm committed to Jacob, but you left me love notes and roses anyway, and now you're trying to *lie* about it."

Shawn's face had gone pink. "Look, I've been taken off the case. I figured that would make you happy. I just came to apologize for threatening your business. That's it. I don't regret anything else."

Anger flashed through me. "Oh, so you're not sorry you made me uncomfortable?"

"I was shooting my shot," he said. "What do you expect me to do, sit back when it's so clear you're unhappy with Jacob?"

"I'm not unhappy with Jacob," I snapped. "I'm in love with Jacob, and frankly, you're acting really—"

A crow cawed somewhere overhead, and I flinched, my gaze shifting to the cloudy sky. A black speck swept across it, heading westward.

Westward. Huh, but that's in—

"Look, I did what I'm supposed to do. I apologized."

"I don't accept your apology," I said, my gaze snapping back to his face. "I don't like how you've been acting. I thought you were a nice guy, Shawn, and—"

"You know what they say about nice guys," Shawn said. "They finish last. I didn't want to finish last, so yeah. Do you have any idea how difficult it is to be the friendly cop who everybody sees as nothing but that? I wanted to be seen as my own person. As a man. A man that maybe you would want."

"Me and every other woman you gave a rose to in town," I said. "Leave me alone, Shawn. I wanted to maintain a healthy friendship with you, but since you can't do that, since you clearly want more than I can offer, I'm telling you to leave me alone. For good."

Shawn's expression morphed into one of pain, and then he took a step back. "You don't mean that."

"I do."

"But—"

Tires crunched on the dirt road, and a police squad car rolled up. The door opened, and a slim woman with dark skin, her hair tied back from her face, stepped out. She was dressed neat as a pin, wearing a pair of sunglasses and carrying identification.

"Detective Carter," she said. "I thought you were taken off the case."

"I was, Detective Turner." His reply was snippy. "I was leaving."

"Good," the new detective said. "Wouldn't want you to continue making Miss Romano here uncomfortable."

Shawn hesitated, he opened his mouth as if to say something, but then strode off toward his car, parked in front of the yard.

Detective Turner watched him every step of the way, her brow creased. She waited until he had gotten into his car before approaching me. "Miss Gina Romano," she said. "Detective Susan Turner. Nice to meet you."

"Detective." I shook her hand.

"We haven't met, but I've heard a lot about you," Detective Turner said. "Specifically about Shawn's treatment of you. I'm sorry that happened, but needless to say, he's taking time off. I'm here to pick up the slack."

"That's great." But the jury was out on how great it would be. Detective Turner might be a stickler for following the rules and not having people interfere in her investigations. Shawn had given me leeway, even if that leeway had come with consequences.

"I would love to talk with you about what you know about the deaths of Beau and Thea," Detective Turner said. "Do you have a minute?"

"Sure," I said, a little dubious.

"Great. Let's sit in my car."

I followed her to the squad. It smelled of leather, paper, and of a flowery perfume.

"What do you want to know, Detective?"

"Everything you can tell me. This case has reached a dead-end because of Detective Carter's poor work. I want help and information, and from what I've heard around town, you're the woman to talk to about that."

I colored. "All right. So, here's the deal…" I told her everything I had found, trying not to leave anything out. I included my suspicions about Shawn, Romeo Moretti, and Joanie, who was Thea's estranged sister. I left out the crow attack, as that seemed like more of a personal issue between the crow and me at this point.

Turner listened and took notes, pausing to ask me for clarification here or there. "This is great, Miss Romano. Thank you. I've got a lot to start with here. It's not like our case files were stacked with information."

"Anything I can do to help."

"You should know that Shawn was at the police station, in full view of other officers and cameras at the time of Beau's murder, however."

That gave him an alibi and cleared him of suspicion. But then why had Thea been holding the rose? Was it possible that the rose was a coincidence?

Detective Turner thanked me for my time, and I got out of her car and headed back inside to tell Jacob about what had happened, my insides twisting with excitement.

A new detective who seemed friendly and open to help. And I'd told Shawn where to shove his roses. More important, one of my suspects was clear.

That left just Joanie and Romeo.

And I had a hunch I knew who to talk to about Romeo.

Twenty-One

Lou and Sasha strolled into Romano's Family Restaurant later that night, arm-in-arm and laughing hysterically about something or the other that had happened to them. It was nice to see smiling faces after the past couple of days.

Then again, I'd have taken anything over crow pecking and caws.

I was so close to solving this mystery, I could taste the rewarding victory pizza Jacob and I would eat to celebrate right afterward.

Lou and Sasha stopped at the hostess stand. "You called?" Lou gave me a winning smile.

"We love that this is your choice of meeting place," Sasha put in. "Particularly since we get to eat Italian food while you question us."

I laughed. "The table by the window is ours," I said. "Don't worry, I won't take much of your time."

"Take all the time you need, Gina. Gosh, you've done so much for the town," Lou said. "It would be mad dumb to say no to you."

"Totally."

The pair went over to the table to take a seat, and I took a breath. I hadn't thought about asking Sasha about Romeo before because, well, the leads had led me in several directions, and I had been sufficiently distracted by the Basil Buzzer and Beau's passing. I could only hope that this would be the clue I was looking for.

I pulled Charles aside, smiling as he dipped down to listen to me intently, and ordered a bottle of red and garlic bread for the table.

I joined Lou and Sasha, stopping to pour them a glass of sparkling water first.

"All right," Sasha said, leaning her chin on top of her fist. "So, what do you wanna know?"

"It's totally about your love life with Romeo," Lou said. "Or lack thereof." He rolled his eyes heavenward.

"I guess you could say he's right," I started.

"He is *not* right. I do not have a lack of a love life." Sasha flicked her long pretty braids over her shoulder.

Lou gave her a grin. "Oh relax, honey, you know I'm just messing with you."

Sasha gave him a look then fluttered her eyelashes. "Anyway, what do you want to know about Romeo?"

"I have a specific question," I said.

Charles delivered the wine and garlic bread to the table, and I waited for Lou and Sasha to help themselves before continuing.

"Oh my gosh, this is the best garlic bread I've ever tasted," Sasha said.

"I'm not even going to regret how much weight I'm gaining," Lou put in. "I can feel the calories in this." He took a bite and relished it. "So good."

"I'm glad you like it," I said, as I poured all of us glasses of wine. "Look, here's the deal. I need to know more about Romeo's movements lately. Specifically on the morning of Beau's death."

"On the morning of Beau's..." Lou trailed off taking a sip of wine to wash down the question. "Well, I have no idea. I didn't see Romeo that morning."

Sasha bit on her bottom lip and glanced down. "Romeo's not in trouble, is he?"

"Not yet," I said. "Do you—Look, I know Lou was kidding the other day about you two dating."

"I believe I said she was practically Romeo's shadow," Lou said happily.

Sasha rolled her eyes at him.

"I know he was kidding around," I said, "but are you an item? And if you are, do you maybe know where he was on the morning that Beau died?"

Because on the morning of Thea's death, Romeo had *definitely* been standing over the body. Notably, he hadn't been covered in blood. I wasn't an expert on blood spatter, but I had figured that surely some blood would've come into contact with Moretti's shirt and jacket? He'd been clean and well-groomed when I'd given him a ride on the morning of Thea's murder.

Darn, I should've asked Detective Turner if she found a change of clothes or why there wasn't spatter. Shawn hadn't told me anything.

"Sasha?" Lou was frowning at his friend.

She continued gnawing on her bottom lip. "Look," she said, "we're not dating, OK? But I—I like him, and I—"

"What?" Lou asked. "You're acting weird."

"I may or may not have been kind of following him around," she said. "I know it's not right, but he—He's been giving me mixed signals."

"I didn't realize he'd been giving you any signals," Lou said. "I thought he was just a crush. Wait. Oh my gosh," Lou said. "Is that the reason you wanted us to have breakfast at the guesthouse on the morning of Thea's murder?"

Sasha bowed her head.

"But wait," Lou said. "How did you even know he was there in the first place?"

A great question.

"I may or may not have put a tracking app on his phone when he came by the library the other day," Sasha said.

"That is... wild, Sasha," Lou said. "And seriously not OK."

"I know," she said. "I know. It was the wrong thing to do, but I guess I just — He's so cute. And he keeps telling me I'm pretty, and then I heard a rumor that he was giving other girls in town roses or something."

Roses? Not *more* roses. Unless Sasha's wires were crossed about Shawn's rose endeavors. "OK, wait, you had an app on his phone tracking him. So, then you know where he was on the morning of Beau's murder," I said.

"Yeah."

"And?" Lou shook his head, taking a sip of his wine. "Come on, Sasha, spit it out. We're dying over here."

"He was at Moretti's Italian Restaurant," she said. "With some guys. I drove over there and looked, and he was with some other men."

I let out a breath. Romeo hadn't killed Beau.

"OK, great," Lou said. "But you need to delete that app like... yesterday."

"No wait," I said. "Keep it. Keep it and give that information to Detective Turner. She'll want to know, and that could be super valuable for her."

Because it would set her on the same path as me.

With the new information that Joanie was Thea's estranged sister, there was only one suspect left on my list.

Twenty-Two

THE CROW.

The crow had perched on top of our house. I sat in the Lexus, staring up at it through narrowed eyes.

What was it with this bird? Why had it taken such a dislike to me?

I'd left the restaurant after my lunch chat with Lou and Sasha. I'd been taking off more time than usual, and while I trusted Charles and Vi to run the place while I was gone, and that Jacob and his chefs would continue their top-notch performance, I felt uneasy about it. I was a hands-on owner, and I liked to be around in my restaurant, making sure that customers were happy.

But the mystery had consumed me.

Joanie had to be the culprit. Right? But how was I going to prove it?

More importantly, how was I going to get out of my car without getting attacked?

I rolled down my window a tiny bit and glared up at the crow. "You know," I said, "I don't usually have problems with animals. I treat all of them equally. I love nature. So why are you being such—?"

"Shoo!" The crow said, black feathers lifting and settling.

I shivered. "You shoo. You're the one on my property!"

"Shoo," the crow repeated.

"No. You shoo. You!" I was tempted to lay on the horn. "I'm not the one who attacked you, if you rem—" I cut off my eyes widening.

It couldn't be a coincidence, could it?

The crow.

The crow being here, then being at Moretti's. The crow chasing and pecking me when I'd approached Joanie's house, and then it had been — "At the guesthouse."

And the other day, I'd seen it flying off over the houses along the lake. Didn't crows usually travel in groups?

It's called a murder of crows for a reason.

"You belong to her, don't you?" I asked.

"Keep a lookout," the crow replied, before taking flight and soaring off over the trees in the direction of Joanie's house.

I gasped, the realization so stark my hand jolted where I'd placed it on the steering wheel and I accidentally pressed the horn.

On the day Beau had been murdered, I'd been distracted by the crow. It had left the oak tree, screeching and making a noise as if *to warn somebody.* And shortly after, I'd heard the slam of a door inside.

But was I right about the crow belonging to Joanie?

I had to find out. But first, I had to make a quick call.

THE TUBE OF PEPPER SPRAY HEATED UP FAST IN my palm, possibly because I was so darn sweaty. If I could prove that the crow belonged to Joanie, and find another shred of evidence, anything, that linked her to the crime scene...

I'd done the responsible thing and put in a call to Detective Turner, who'd given me her number specifically in case anything like this popped up.

You can do this.

I crept through the woods, switching my gaze from the rough bark, the spaces between the trunks, and up to the canopy above. It was afternoon, so making out the shape of a crow in the foliage should've been easy.

The last thing I wanted was to run into the crow again and deal with more dive-bombing, cawing and trouble.

I continued the even pace, checking everywhere as I moved and hoping that the information I'd given the detective would be enough for her to at least interrogate her. If they got a warrant for Joanie's house, even better.

After all, I'd done my due diligence.

Unless, of course, I'd missed a suspect during my evaluation of the suspect list. I couldn't think about that now.

Finally, I reached the treeline that looked out on the back of Joanie's house. The house was silent, but the crow sat on the gabled roof, its beady eyes studying the lawn below.

A door slammed, and Joanie emerged from the back of the house, striding across the grass in her long cape. "Raven," she called.

The crow took flight, and Joanie held out her arm. It landed atop it.

"There's a good boy," she said. "You've been a good look out today."

"Look out!"

"That's right." Joanie cooed and stroked its beak and black feathered head. This would have been a cute scene if the crow hadn't attacked me, and I wasn't convinced that Joanie was the murderer. "You've been such a good friend lately, Raven. I've only got one more thing for you to do."

Joanie produced a golden chain from her pocket and held it out to her pet crow.

The bird took flight and grabbed the chain in its talons. It flew toward the trees.

Exactly in line with my hiding spot.

Hurriedly, I ducked out of sight then lifted my gaze to the leaves overhead.

The crow swept over them, and I turned and followed it as quietly as I could. It didn't go far, about five trees deep into the woods, and settled into the nest it had built in the nook between two branches of an old oak.

I waited and finally, the crow took flight again, heading back in the direction of Joanie's house.

Silence.

Was I really going to do this?

It had been a long time since I'd climbed a tree. I tucked my pepper spray into my left pocket, my phone into my right. Thankfully, the oak had plenty of branches. I only slipped a couple of times on my way up.

This had to be at the top of the list of the most ridiculous things I had done, and that was saying a lot since I'd recently pepper sprayed a murderer.

I reached the nest, wedging my feet on the branch below and craning my neck to get a glimpse of what else the crow had hidden inside.

My heart leaped in my chest and my stomach sank shortly afterward.

There was a stubby yet sharp knife in the nest. The blade was stained with blood.

I had it. I had the murder weapon.

Carefully, I balanced on the branch, one hand pressed against the tree trunk, and extracted my phone. I snapped a picture of the knife and sent it to Detective Turner's phone.

Already on our way out there. Drop me a pin so I can send an officer out to you. Stay where you are and out of sight.

Got it. Thanks, Detective.

Thank you for your help, Gina.

A smile parted my lips.

It had been worth it. The random roses. The worry. The "being pecked half-to-death by a crow" part, because the police were on their way.

And Joanie was going to get what she deserved. A long sentence behind bars.

Twenty-Three

"It's down," Matilda announced from the kitchen table. "They finally took it down."

"That's a relief," Aunt Sofia said. "That website just made me sad. All those lies. And poor Beau who created it in the first place is gone."

"They weren't all lies," Uncle Rocco said, and took a sip of his beer. "Think about it. Beau posted the right information about that crazy crow lady."

I smiled at Uncle Rocco from where I stood beside Jacob, chopping up ingredients for our pizza night. "Yeah, I guess you're right, Uncle. She did have a criminal past—but there weren't any warrants out for her arrest. Otherwise I'm sure Shawn or Detective Turner would have arrested her."

Uncle Rocco grumbled. He wasn't entirely sure about

that. He'd been furious when he'd found out about Shawn's inappropriate behavior toward me.

Jacob slipped his arm around my waist and gave me a side-hug while he waited for the oven to heat up.

It was a cold fall night, and it was perfect for a family dinner. Jumbo meowed from Matilda's lap, while Uncle Rocco and Aunt Sof chatted to her about how things were going in the bakery. The atmosphere was warm and happy.

This was so different from how life had been when I'd first arrived in Lake Basil, and it made me ridiculously happy.

Music played from our stereo on the counter in the corner, and Uncle Rocco would occasionally wiggle in time to the music or nod his head and tap his hands on the table.

Jacob poured everyone a round of their favorite drinks while I dipped to the restroom.

Halfway down the hall, a clatter from the study near the front of the house drew my attention.

I sucked in a breath then released it.

After the craziness of the past couple of months, I was tense, but this would be nothing. Surely, it wouldn't be another rose or message from Shawn. He had given up at last, especially now that a lot of women in town were talking about how he had courted them as well. And they'd been angry about it.

I entered the study and flicked the light-switch on the wall.

The window was open a crack, and the black cat who'd been frequenting our bushes lately stood just inside the window, bright yellow eyes wide.

It meowed at me.

"Hello, kitty," I said. "Do you want to come in and rest?"

A second meow, tentative.

"I'll get you some water and food." We'd gotten some from the store just in case the kitty came back. I went to the kitchen and grabbed what I needed, mentioning it to Jacob on the way. He excused himself from the kitchen and followed me.

"There, there, kitty," he said. "Come on down."

The cat stayed where it was, watching us with wary eyes as we put out water and food for it. We didn't want to upset Jumbo, but if we kept the study door closed, the two cats wouldn't encounter each other.

Jacob and I hovered by the door for a second, watching the cat as it eyed the food bowl from its perch on the windowsill.

We closed the door and exited into the hall. Jacob started toward the kitchen, but I grabbed hold of his forearm and stopped him.

"Honey," I said. "Wait."

"What's up?" Jacob smiled at me.

"I saw what you were looking at earlier in the week."

"Huh?"

"Rings," I said. "I saw you were looking at engagement rings on your phone."

"Oh." Jacob cleared his throat. "Yeah, I—Look, I don't want to scare you, but—"

"I'm not afraid," I said.

"You're not?"

"No," I replied. "If you're interested in looking at rings, then so am I."

Jacob's handsome face broke into a smile that showed off his dimples. He chuckled. "Gina, are you saying that you want to marry me?"

"I'm saying that I wouldn't be opposed to it," I said. "You're the one for me, Jacob, and even though the thought of getting engaged is... well, it brings back bad memories of the past, I want to make all new memories with you."

Jacob swept me into a hug and squeezed me tight. "Great," he said. "Then maybe I will look at a few rings. Maybe I won't. We'll see."

"Keeping me on my toes, huh?"

He kissed me gently then stepped back. "You bet," he said. "A woman like you needs to be kept on her toes. You like excitement."

"Me?" I pressed a hand to my chest, pretending to be scandalized. "Whatever would make you think that?"

Jacob laughed and took me by the hand. We entered the kitchen to find Uncle Rocco and Matilda in a heated debate about whether America or the United Kingdom had the better baked goods.

"Scones," Matilda said, slapping the table. "You can't argue with scones."

"Yeah, you can. You never had a cannoli before?"

"But cannolis aren't American," Matilda said.

Aunt Sofia gave a scandalized gasp.

"What?" Matilda glanced between the two of them. "They're not. They're Sicilian."

"Fine, then what about pancakes?"

"Crepes are from France," Matilda said.

"What are you, British?" Uncle Rocco grumbled.

"I'm American, thank you very much," she replied, "but the facts are the facts. I mean, scones, crumpets, spotted dick pudding."

Aunt Sofia clapped her hand over her mouth, her eyes going wide.

Uncle Rocco's neck pinked.

"It's a suet pudding," Matilda said quickly. "With dried fruit. Served with custard."

"Ah!" Uncle Rocco held up a finger, sweeping it

through the air. "Chocolate chip cookies. Best baked goods in history."

Matilda wriggled her nose left and right. "All right. I'll concede on that point."

"Ha. Can't beat a good chocolate chip cookie."

Jacob and I returned to our cooking, preparing the toppings for the pizza, occasionally sharing a secret smile or a chuckle at Matilda and Uncle Rocco's ongoing debates.

It had been a rough couple of weeks, but this was our reward. Time with our family, with Jumbo occasionally stealing bits of ham from the floor. Whatever came next in our lives, whether it was getting engaged or more mysteries to solve, we'd be ready for it. Together.

Will Gina and Jacob finally get engaged? What other strange occurrences will Gina and her friends encounter in Lake Basil? And what exactly is Romeo Moretti planning with his shady friends?

Find out in THE CONCHIGLIE CATASTROPHE.

Craving More Cozy Mystery?

If you had fun with Ruby and Bee, you'll, love getting to know Charlie Mission and her butt-kicking grandmother, Georgina. You can read the first chapter of Charlie's story, *The Case of the Waffling Warrants,* below!

"Come in, Big G, come in." I spoke under my breath so that the flesh-colored microphone seated against my throat picked up my voice. "What is your status?"

My grandmother, Georgina—pet name Gamma, code name Big G—was out on a special operation. Reconnaissance at the newest guesthouse in our town, Gossip. The reason? First, she was an ex-spy, as was I, and second, the woman who'd opened the guesthouse was her mortal enemy and in direct competition with my grandmother's establishment, the Gossip Inn.

Who was this enemy, this bringer of potential financial doom?

A middle-aged woman with a penchant for wearing pashminas and annoying anyone who looked her way.

Jessie Belle-Blue.

It was rumored that even thinking the woman's name summoned a murder of crows.

"I repeat, Big G, what is your status?"

"I'm en route to the nest," my grandmother replied in my earpiece.

I let out a relieved sigh and exited my bedroom, heading downstairs to help with the breakfast service.

In the nine months since I had retired as a spy, life in Gossip had been normal. In the Gossip sense of the term. I'd expected that my job as a server, maid, and assistant would bring the usual level of "cat herding" inherent when working at the inn. Whether that involved tracking down runaway cats, literally, or providing a guest with a moist towelette after a fainting spell—tempers ran high in Gossip.

What was the reason for the craziness? Shoot, it had to be something in the water.

I took the main stairs two at a time and found my friend, the inn's chef, paging through her recipe book in the lime green kitchen. Lauren Harris wore her red hair in a French braid today, apron stretched over her pregnant belly.

"Morning," I said, "how are you today?"

"Madder than a fat cat on a diet." She slapped her recipe book closed and turned to me.

Uh oh. Looks like it's time for more cat herding.

"What's wrong?"

"My supplier is out of flour and sugar. Can you believe that?" Lauren huffed, smoothing her hands over her belly while the clock on the wall ticked away. Breakfast was in two hours and Lauren loved baking cupcakes as part of the meal.

"Do you have enough supplies to make cupcakes for this morning?"

"Yes. But just for today," Lauren replied. "The guests are going to love my new waffle cupcakes, and they'll be sore they can't get anymore after this batch is done. Why, I should go down there and wring Billy's neck for doing this to me. He knows I take an order of sugar and flour every week, and I get it at just above cost too. What's Georgina going to say?"

"Don't stress, Lauren," I said. "We'll figure it out."

"Right." She brightened a little. "I nearly forgot you're the one who "fixes" things around here." Lauren winked at me.

She was the only person in the entire town who knew that my grandmother and I had once been spies for the NSIB—the National Security Investigative Bureau. But the news that I had helped solve several murders had spread through town, and now, anybody and everybody with a problem would call me up asking for help. A lot of them offered me money. And I was selective about who I chose to help.

"I'll check it out for you if you'd like," I said. "The flour issue."

"Nah, that's OK. I'm sure Billy will get more stock this week. I'll lean on him until he squeals."

"Sounds like you've been picking up tips from Georgina."

Lauren giggled then returned to her super-secret recipe book—no one but she was allowed to touch it.

"What's on the menu this morning?" I asked.

Lauren was the boss in the kitchen—she told me what to do, and I followed her instructions precisely. If I did anything else, like trying to read the recipe for instance, the food would end up burned, missing ingredients or worse.

The only place I wasn't a "fixer" was in the Gossip Inn's kitchen.

"Bacon and eggs over easy, biscuits and gravy, waffle cupcakes and... oh, I can't make fresh baked bread, can I?"

"Tell her I'll bring some back with me from the

bakery." Gamma's voice startled me. Goodness, I'd forgotten about the earpiece—she could hear everything happening in the kitchen.

"I'll text Georgina and ask her to bring bread from the bakery."

"You're a lifesaver, Charlotte."

We set to work on the breakfast—it was 7:00 a.m. and we needed everything done within two hours—and fell into our easy rhythm of baking and cooking.

My grandmother entered the kitchen at around 8:30 a.m., dressed in a neat silk blouse and a pair of slacks rather than the black outfit she'd left in for her spy mission. Tall, willowy, and with neatly styled gray hair, Gamma had always reminded me of Helen Mirren playing the Queen.

"Good morning, ladies," she said, in her prim, British accent. "I bring bread and tidings."

"What did you find out?" I asked.

"No evidence of the supposed ghost tours," Gamma said.

We'd started hosting ghost tours at the inn recently, so of course Jessie Belle-Blue wanted to do the same. She was all about under-cutting us, but, thankfully, the Gossip Inn had a legacy and over 1,000 positive reviews on Trip-Advisor.

Breakfast time arrived, and the guests filled the quaint dining area with its glossy tables, creaking wooden floors, and egg yolk yellow walls. Chatter and laughter leaked through the swinging kitchen doors with their porthole windows.

"That's my cue," I said, dusting off my apron, and heading out into the dining room.

I picked up a pot of coffee from the sideboard where we kept the drinks station and started my rounds.

Most of the guests had gathered around a center table in the dining room, and bursts of laughter came from the group, accompanied by the occasional shout.

I elbowed my way past a couple of guests—nobody could accuse me of having great people skills—apologizing along the way until I reached the table. The last time something like this had happened, a murder had followed shortly afterward.

Not this time. No way.

"—the last thing she'd ever hear!" The woman seated at the table, drawing the attention, was vaguely familiar. She wore her dark hair in luscious curls, and tossed it as she spoke, looking down her upturned nose at the people around the table.

"What happened then, Mandy?" Another woman asked, her hands clasped together in front of her stomach.

Mandy? Wait a second, isn't this Mandy Gilmore?

Gamma had mentioned her once before—Mandy was

a massive gossip in town. Why wasn't she staying at her house?

"What happened? Well, she ran off with her tail between her legs, of course. She'll soon learn not to cross me. Heaven knows, I always repay my debts."

"What, like a Lannister from *Game of Thrones*?" That had come from a taller woman with ginger curls.

"Shut up, Opal," Mandy replied. "You have no idea what we're talking about, and even if you did, you wouldn't have the intelligence to comprehend it."

The crowd let out various 'oofs' in response to that. The woman next to me clapped her hand over her mouth.

"You're all talk, Gilmore." Opal lifted a hand and yammered it at the other woman. "You act like you're a threat, but we know the truth around here."

"The truth?" Mandy leaned in, pressing her hands flat onto the tabletop, the crystal vase in the center rattling. "And what's that, Opal, darling? I'd love to hear it."

"That you're a failure. You sold your house, left Gossip with your head in the clouds, told everyone you were going to become a successful businesswoman, and now you're back. Back to scrape together the pieces of the life you have left."

"Witch!" Mandy scraped her chair back.

"All right, all right," I said, setting down the coffee pot

on the table. "That's enough, ladies. Everyone head back to their tables before things get out of hand."

Both Opal and Mandy stared daggers at me.

I flashed them both smiles. "We wouldn't want to ruin breakfast, would we? Lauren's prepared waffle cupcakes."

That distracted them. "Waffle cupcakes?" Opal's brow wrinkled. "How's that going to work?"

"Let's talk about it at your table." I grabbed my coffee pot and walked her away from Mandy. The crowd slowly dispersed, people muttering regret at having missed out on a show. The Gossip Inn was popular for its constant conflict.

If the rumors didn't start here then they weren't worth repeating. That was the mantra, anyway.

I seated Opal at her table, and she pursed her lips at me. "You shouldn't have interrupted. That woman needs a piece of my mind."

"We prefer peace of mind at the inn." I put up another of my best smiles.

Compared to what I'd been through in the past—hiding out from my rogue spy ex-husband and eventually helping put him behind bars when he found me—dealing with the guests was a cakewalk.

"What brings you to Gossip, Opal?" I asked.

"I live here," she replied, waspishly. "I'm staying here while they're fumigating my house. Roaches."

"Ah." I struggled not to grimace. Thankfully, my cell phone buzzed in the front pocket of my apron and distracted me. "Coffee?"

"I don't take caffeine." And she said it like I'd offered her an illegal substance too.

"Call me if you need anything." I hurried off before she could make good on that promise, bringing my phone out of my pocket.

I left the coffee pot on the sideboard, moving into the Gossip Inn's spacious foyer, the chandelier overhead off, but catching light in glimmers. The tables lining the hall were filled with trinkets from the days when the inn had been a museum—an eclectic collection of bits and bobs.

"This is Charlotte Smith," I answered the call—I would never get to use my true last name, Mission, again, but it was safer this way.

"Hello, Charlotte." A soft, rasping voice. "I've been trying to get through to you. I'm desperate."

"Who is this?"

"My name is Tina Rogers, and I need your help."

"My help."

"Yes," she said. "I understand that you have a certain set of skills. That you fix people's problems?"

"I do. But it depends on the problem and the price." I didn't have a set fee for helping people, but if it drew me away from the inn for long, I had to charge. I was technically a consultant now. Sort of like a P.I. without the fedora and coffee-stained shirt.

"My mother will handle your fee," Tina said. "I've asked her to text you about it, but I... I don't have long to talk. They're going to pull me off the phone soon."

"Who?"

"The police," she replied. "I'm calling you from the holding cell at the Gossip Police Station. I've been arrested on false charges, and I need you to help me prove my innocence."

"Miss Rogers, it's probably a better idea to invest in a lawyer." But I was tempted. It had been a long time since I'd felt useful.

"No! I'm not going to a lawyer. I'm going to make these idiots pay for ever having arrested me."

I took a breath. "OK. Before I accept your... case, I'll need to know what happened. You'll need to tell me every-thing." I glanced through the open doorway that led into the dining room. No one looked unhappy about the lack of service yet.

"I can't tell you everything now. I don't have much time."

"So give me the *CliffsNotes*."

"I was arrested for breaking into and vandalizing Josie Carlson's bakery, The Little Cake Shop. Apparently, they found my glove there—it was specially embroidered, you see—but it's not mine because—" The line went dead.

"Hello? Miss Rogers?" I pulled the cellphone away from my ear and frowned at the screen. "Darn."

My interest was piqued. A mystery case about a break-in that involved the local bakery? Which just so happened to be run by one of my least favorite people in Gossip?

And when I'd just started getting bored with the push and pull of everyday life at the inn?

Count me in.

Want to read more? You can grab **the first book** in *the Gossip Cozy Mystery series* on all major retailers.

Happy reading, friend!

Murder With Sprinkles

Trick or Murder

Christmas Cake Murder

S'more Murder

Murder and Marshmallows

Donut Murder

Buttercream Murder

Chocolate Cherry Murder

Caramel Apple Murder

Red, White 'n Blue Murder

Pink Sprinkled Murder

Murder by Milkshake

Murder by Cupid Cake

Caramel Cupcake Murder

Cake Pops and Murder

A Milly Pepper Mystery series

Maple Drizzle Murder

A Sunny Side Up Cozy Mystery series

Murder Over Easy

Muffin But Murder

Chicken Murder Soup

Murderoni and Cheese

Lemon Murder Pie

<u>*A Gossip Cozy Mystery series*</u>

The Case of the Waffling Warrants

The Case of the Key Lime Crimes

The Case of the Custard Conspiracy

The Case of the Butterscotch Burglars

<u>*A Mission Inn-possible Cozy Mystery series*</u>

Vanilla Vendetta

Strawberry Sin

Cocoa Conviction

Mint Murder

Raspberry Revenge

Chocolate Chills

<u>*A Very Murder Christmas series*</u>

Dachshund Through the Snow

Owl Be Home for Christmas

<u>*A Pizza Parlor Cozy Mystery series*</u>

Slice of Murder

Murder Boxed Up

Hold the Murder

Dough Not Murder

<u>*A Romano's Family Cozy Mystery series*</u>

The Cannelloni Corpse

The Ravioli Rub Out